She couldn't let him leave—

Not without warning him of the shock that awaited him at his apartment!

"Jake," she began. "I'm afraid you aren't going to be pleased when you get home. In fact," she added miserably, "you will be very angry indeed." She gestured helplessly, not knowing how to explain that she and her friends had decided he'd lied about his promise to save Mrs. Peters's land—and they'd sent him an unforgettable reminder.

"What have you done now? Burned down the apartment building?"

"No of course not. Arson's a felony—"

"Oh great!" he cut in. "Okay, I guess I'll find out soon enough what genius idea you've come up with this time. So just leave me in suspense. Otherwise it's very likely that I'll be found guilty—here and now—of murder!"

MARY LYONS is happily married to an Essex farmer, has two children and lives in an old Victorian rectory. Life is peaceful—unlike her earlier years when she worked as a radio announcer, reviewed books and even ran for Parliament in a London dockland area. She still loves a little excitement and combines romance with action and suspense in her books whenever possible.

Books by Mary Lyons

HARLEQUIN PRESENTS
625—THE PASSIONATE ESCAPE
673—CARIBBEAN CONFUSION
701—DESIRE IN THE DESERT
714—SPANISH SERENADE
763—DANGEROUS STUNT
779—LOVE'S TANGLED WEB
796—MENDED ENGAGEMENT
828—ECLIPSE OF THE HEART

These books may be available at your local bookseller.

Don't miss any of our special offers. Write to us at the following address for information on our newest releases.

Harlequin Reader Service
901 Fuhrmann Blvd., P.O. Box 1397, Buffalo, NY 14240
Canadian address: P.O. Box 2800, Postal Station A,
5170 Yonge St., Willowdale, Ont. M2N 6J3

MARY LYONS

passionate deception

Harlequin Books

TORONTO • NEW YORK • LONDON
AMSTERDAM • PARIS • SYDNEY • HAMBURG
STOCKHOLM • ATHENS • TOKYO • MILAN

Harlequin Presents first edition August 1986
ISBN 0-373-10908-3

Original hardcover edition published in 1986
by Mills & Boon Limited

CHAPTER ONE

THE battered Ford Transit van moved slowly through the crowded streets of the City, turning into Moorgate and passing the Stock Exchange before coming to a halt outside a large modern office block.

A young man sitting in the passenger seat looked doubtfully out of the window. 'Are you sure this is the right place, Harry?'

'Absolutely certain. I drove past here yesterday, just to make sure that everything would go according to plan.' Harriet pulled on the hand brake, cut the engine and pointed to a small, discreet brass plaque set in the wall beside the entrance to the building. 'There—you see? This place might look like the last word in respectability, Andrew,' she added drily, 'but I can assure you that it's definitely the London headquarters of Lancaster International.'

'Okay, so what do we do now?'

Harriet released her seat belt and turned to face the speaker, a short girl with a mop of blonde curls, who was sitting perched uncomfortably on the lap of one of the three male students squashed into the rear seat.

'I only managed to paint four placards last night,' she explained. 'And since they're quite heavy, I thought we'd let the guys carry them . . .'

'So kind!' Andrew muttered.

'. . . while you and I, Rosie, hand out the leaflets,' Harriet continued with a grin. 'We'll have to get a move on. Not only is this van parked on double yellow lines, and we need the attention of a traffic warden like a hole in the head, but the meeting is due to begin in under an

5

hour. So, if you'll all get out and remove the placards
and leaflets from the rear of the van, I'll look for a
place to park this dump on wheels, and be back to join
you as soon as I can.'

Rejoining her companions some minutes later, they
decided, after some discussion, that the boys would
stand in pairs either side of the entrance, while Rosie
and she divided the leaflets between them.

'Now do remember—this is supposed to be a peaceful
protest,' Harriet cautioned her fellow students. 'Just as
long as we make sure that we don't obstruct the
pavement, we have a perfect right to be here and we are
not breaking the law.'

'These are really great—absolutely brilliant!' exclaimed Rosie, who had been reading one of the
leaflets. 'Do we hand them out to every single person
entering the building?'

Harriet hesitated, wondering what was their best
course of action. 'Well, at this time of the afternoon,
I'm willing to bet that ninety-nine per cent of the people
going through that door, will be shareholders coming to
attend the Annual General Meeting,' she said. 'In any
case, it can't hurt the people who work here to find out
just what dastardly deeds are being carried out by their
employers! I reckon that we ought to make sure that we
don't miss anyone—what do you think, Andrew?'

'No one is going to be able to miss you, Harry—not
in that outfit you're wearing!' He gave a deep, mocking
groan, dramatically throwing up an arm to shield his
eyes from the sight of her tall, slim figure. 'Why, *oh
why*, didn't I bring my sun-glasses?' he moaned.

Standing six foot high in her stockinged feet,
Harriet's bright chestnut, wavy hair fell in a thick cloud
about her shoulders. It violently clashed with, and
provided a startling contrast to, the shimmering satin,
cerise pink blouse tucked into skin-tight scarlet jeans;

the whole 'ensemble' terminating in bright canary
yellow, high-heeled cowboy boots.

'Yes, it's really awful, isn't it?' she laughed, busily
handing out leaflets to the steady stream of people
arriving for the meeting, most of whom blinked with
astonishment, both at what they read on the placards
and at the extraordinary vision of Harriet standing
before them.

'Still, that's the whole object of this first part of the
exercise,' she added, beaming happily at an elderly man
who was regarding her with dazed eyes. 'It's important
that everyone looks at my clothes, and not at my face. I
want to make absolutely sure that the great Mr Jason
Lancaster, of Lancaster International, has a *very*
uncomfortable afternoon!'

Mr Jason Lancaster—known to his friends, colleagues
and fiancée as Jake—the Chairman and Managing
Director of Lancaster International was, at that precise
moment, seated very comfortably in the back seat of his
chauffeur-driven Rolls Royce. The day had not begun
auspiciously. His flight from Paris had been unaccount-
ably delayed, and for a time it had looked as if he
would be late for his company's Annual General
Meeting. Now, however, as he glanced at his watch,
and then looked out of the car window to note the
dome of St Paul's Cathedral towering above the other
City buildings, he saw that his chauffeur had indeed
followed his instructions to 'step on it' when he had
picked up his employer at Heathrow airport.

'Well done, Benson,' he said, putting the financial
reports he had been reading back into the briefcase on
the seat beside him. 'After you've dropped me at the
office, you can take my bags over to the apartment and
tell Carter that . . .' Jake paused as the Rolls slowed
down outside the office block owned by his company,

his hard blue eyes narrowing at the sight of a large,
agitated group of people milling about the entrance to
the building. Swiftly recovering from his surprise he
realised, from the raised placards at the back of the
crowd, that some sort of demonstration seemed to be in
progress. He was too far away to read the words
painted on the large boards, but his mouth tightened
with annoyance as his chauffeur continued around the
corner and down into the underground car park.

Taking his personal express elevator to the top floor
of the building, Jake strode swiftly through the hushed
reception area and threw open the heavy mahogany
doors of his own palatial office suite. Tossing his
briefcase into one of the red leather arm chairs scattered
about the room, he ignored the flustered enquiries of
his middle-aged personal secretary, Ann Norris.

'Just get me Ross on the 'phone—immediately!' he
snapped, pacing irritably up and down the large room
as his secretary appeared to be experiencing some
difficulty in locating the commissionaire.

'He's just coming,' she murmured a few minutes later,
backing nervously away as he seized the telephone from
her hand.

'What in the hell's going on, Ross?' Jake demanded,
drumming his fingers impatiently on the desk. 'Yes, yes,
I saw them as we drove past the front door . . . Look, I
don't care who they are or what they are supposedly
protesting about, I want them moved away from the
building . . . Well, if you can't manage it on your own,
then call in the police . . . For God's sake—don't argue
with me! Just get rid of them, okay?'

His secretary flinched as he slammed down the
receiver. 'There's obviously a problem of some kind. Is
there anything I can do to help?' she asked.

Jake sighed and ran a hand through his thick dark
hair. 'No. Ross or the police should soon have matters

well under control. I'm sorry if I was a bit abrupt just now, Ann, but it's really been one hell of a day. First I got held up in Paris—and now this!' He gave her a warm, tired smile, shrugging off his dark grey suit jacket and going through to the adjacent bathroom to wash his travel-stained face and hands.

'I still don't understand what's happening,' Ann said as he returned looking more his usual urbane self.

'I wouldn't have believed it if I hadn't seen them with my own eyes,' he gave a harsh bark of laughter. 'We seem to have a demonstration going on outside the front door of this building. It's just a bunch of kids,' he added reassuringly. 'They're undoubtedly making a plea for the starving millions in Africa, or nuclear disarmament, or whatever's the fashionable cause for students this year!'

'But Mr Lancaster,' she looked at him aghast. 'Surely you can't have forgotten that the Annual General Meeting is due to start in half an hour?'

'No, of course I haven't. However, since I am fully confident that either Ross or the local police will have moved them on by now, I suggest that we settle down to some work, hmm? There are one or two points arising from my visit to France that . . .' He looked up with a frown as Sir Humphrey Ellis, a senior director of the company, rushed wildly into the room.

'You've got to come downstairs and sort it all out, Jake. I can't cope with all the questions they're asking—I really can't!' The older man gestured helplessly and collapsed into a leather armchair.

'What on earth are you talking about, Humphrey?' Jake looked at him in astonishment. 'What have I got to "sort out"? Who is asking questions?'

'It's the shareholders. They're arriving thick and fast, and demanding to know why the company's in financial trouble . . .'

Jake gave a contemptuous snort of derision. 'I've never heard such nonsense. We've just declared the best dividend in the Company's history—you must be out of your mind!'

'No . . . I mean, yes—yes, of course you're right. Yes, indeed. But many of the shareholders are now beginning to question our financial report. It's all very . . . very embarrassing.' Sir Humphrey lay back in his chair, wiping the sweat from his forehead with a large white handkerchief.

'Why?' Jake demanded, his hard voice cutting through the temporary silence. 'Tell me just why our shareholders are suddenly dissatisfied with our financial standing?'

'Well, I didn't understand what it was all about—not at first. But then Ross, the commissionaire, came and dragged me through the foyer and outside into the street. My dear chap—that girl! I've never seen anything so horrible . . .!' he shuddered. 'And as for what those placards are saying . . . well, it's libel, or slander, or maybe both for all I know.'

Jake leaned back in his chair. 'Ann, would you be kind enough to give Sir Humphrey a strong whisky, please. Now,' he added as the older man gratefully pressed his trembling hands around the glass of amber liquid. 'Are we talking about our shareholders, or the demonstration which was going on outside this building?'

'Well, it's all one and the same thing, you see.'

'No, I don't!' Jake snapped. 'Surely Ross or the police have got rid of those students by now?'

'Ross called the police, but they were still arguing when I left to come up here. From what I gathered, their ringleader is claiming that they are lawfully and peacefully picketing the building. And the police seem to agree with her—I simply don't understand what's going on.'

'You're not the only one,' Jake retorted grimly. 'Come on—pull yourself together, man! They're only students, for heaven's sake—all you have to do is to go down and deal firmly with them.'

'Oh, no! I'm not facing that—that Amazon again. You can do what you like, but I'm staying right here until the situation has been resolved,' he added defiantly.

'Oh, for God's sake! Isn't there anyone in this building capable of using their initiative?' Jake rose angrily to his feet. 'Okay, it looks as if I'll have to go down and sort out this so-called demonstration. But I think that you and I will have to have a serious talk about your future with this company, Humphrey,' he added ominously, striding swiftly out of the room, and banging the door loudly behind him.

By the time his tall figure had forced his way past the noisy, aggressive crowd of shareholders filling the foyer of the building, and through the press of people jamming the entrance, Jake became aware that, for the first time in many years, he was in serious danger of completely losing his temper. Standing outside on the pavement he gazed up with incredulity at the placards. The signs, hand-painted in bold lettering read:

WHY IS LANCASTER INTERNATIONAL BANKRUPT?

A red mist seemed to cloud his vision, and he had to blink several times before he was able to read the small lettering underneath: 'Morally bankrupt in failing to offer fair and reasonable alternative housing for the occupants of the houses they intend to demolish—to make way for their new housing development in the King's Cross area of London.'

Rigid with fury and still unable to believe his eyes, he became aware of a small, blonde girl placing a piece of paper in his hands. Automatically glancing down, he

saw that he was staring at a photograph of himself. Taken some months ago, it showed him seated at a nightclub, a glass of champagne in hand as he smiled into the eyes of a beautiful woman.

WANTED . . . FOR VICTIMIZATION OF OLD AGE PENSIONER!

JASON   LANCASTER—the   well-known American tycoon and mega-rich banker, can be seen enjoying himself with his latest fiancée, beautiful model, Magda Thorne. Yes, he's certainly having a good time! But does he know or care about the plight of poor Mrs Elsie Peters? His company intends to destroy her home—which is in a very good structural condition—because of his plans to develop a large site, building cheap and very nasty 'rabbit hutchs' for first-time buyers. Lucky Mr Lancaster! He lives in a luxurious penthouse apartment overlooking Hyde Park, so why should he care what happens to Mrs Peters? Or that she was a first-time buyer—over 50 years ago? *Why should she now be made homeless, just to boost the enormous profits of Jason Lancaster and his greedy shareholders?*

With a bellow of rage, Jake spun on his heel, blindly grabbing the arm of a policeman, who with his companion was arguing with Ross the commissionaire.

'Arrest them!' he thundered. 'I demand that you arrest these people, *immediately*!'

'Well, sir, I really don't think that there is a case for me to do so,' the policeman said, quietly and calmly removing Jake's hand from his sleeve.

'What absolute nonsense! They have no right to be here, and . . .'

'Oh, yes we do!'

The high, cool voice cut through his angry words,

and Jake turned to find himself staring into a pair of amused, sparkling grey eyes heavily fringed by thick dark lashes. *Staring straight into, not down* . . . Jake shook his head, reeling from the third or fourth shock he had sustained that day. It wasn't just the fact that, at six feet four inches, he had *never* found himself staring straight into a woman's eyes before, let alone a girl as beautiful as this one appeared to be—but neither had he ever had his visual senses so assaulted. Those violent, clashing colours . . .! Dear God! Surely no one in their right senses would be seen dead wearing clothes like that . . .? Shutting his eyes for a moment, he found himself wildly and feverishly wondering if, by some malign and evil chance, he had somehow strayed into the midst of a hallucinogenic nightmare.

Harriet was enjoying herself. The demo was proving to be a great success, and provoking a far greater response from the shareholders of Lancaster International than she had dared to hope. And to crown it all, here was the big fish himself! Having spent the last week wading through financial papers and magazines, searching for a suitable photograph for reproduction on the leaflet, she had immediately known the identity of the man who was now glaring at her with such hard blue eyes. What an unexpected coup to have managed to entice him into the open! Down here in the street, well away from the shelter and protection of his undoubtedly luxurious office, he was likely to be far more vulnerable.

But how odd that she hadn't realised he would have an American accent? It was surprising, too, how much younger he looked in the flesh. Having done her homework, she knew that he was at least thirty-five, and since she was only twenty-one, she had thought of him as old as Methuselah. It was a bit of a shock to find that he was really was . . . well, quite an extraordinarily good-

looking man—even if he was regarding her with a ferocious scowl, and clearly longing to 'terminate her with extreme prejudice'. She smiled to herself at her use of the ridiculous phrase—allegedly the American C.I.A.'s euphemism for killing people. A smile that prompted Jake to find his voice at last.

'What in the hell do you think you are doing?' he demanded through clenched teeth.

'Mr Jason Lancaster—sometimes known as Jake?' she enquired in a soft voice.

'Yes,' he snapped. 'Now, will you please answer my question? What are you doing here, and do you realise that you can be prosecuted for displaying such slanderous material?' He gestured wildly in the direction of the placards.

'Well . . .' Harriet pretended to consider the matter. 'That's actually two questions, you know.' She gave him a wide, broad smile which she was quite certain he would find almost unbearably irritating. She saw that she was right! From the fierce clenching of his jaw and the sight of a pulse beating wildly at his temple, it looked as if he was going to blow up any minute.

'Now, miss, if you could just explain the position to this gentleman,' the policeman interjected quickly. If he was any judge of people, it looked as if, any minute now, this large man was going to get very nasty.

'Of course, officer, I'm only too pleased to oblige,' she agreed quickly, instantly coming to the same conclusion as the policeman. 'The fact is that we are engaged on a peaceful picket of these premises, and . . .'

'Peaceful picket . . .?' Jake exploded with fury. 'I've never heard such a bare-faced lie!'

Harriet shook her head sorrowfully. 'Oh dear, poor Mr Lancaster—you are confused! First of all, "slander" isn't the right word for the placards. Now, if you had

accused us of "libel", you might be nearer the mark.
Briefly: slander is said, libel is written, okay?'

'No it's damn-well *not* "okay", you—you left-wing
looney! Just wait until I see my lawyer. You'll soon find
out just how non-okay it is!'

'Save your breath—and your money, Mr Lancaster,'
she snapped back. 'I can assure you that those placards
are not actionable, unless you wish to have an argument
in the High Court about the *moral* bankruptcy of your
company. I can't wait to hear the Judge's summing up
in that particular case!

'Now, come along, miss,' the policeman begged.

'Yes, I'm sorry, I was straying off the point,' Harriet
muttered, careful to keep a distance between herself and
Jake's threatening figure. 'To put it very simply: I and
my companions are legally and lawfully within our
rights. All of us hold shares in your company, and
feeling as strongly as we do about some of the decisions
made by the said company, we are drawing attention to
our grievances. Within the terms of the act, we fulfil the
requirements that there shall be no more than six
persons picketing at any one time, and as you can see it
is not we who are impeding the Queen's highway, but
your other shareholders—and indeed you, yourself!'

'Well said, Harry!' Andrew called out, his support
being echoed by the large crowd who had gathered
around Harriet and Jake.

Something seemed to snap in Jake's brain. 'I don't
believe, not for one—minute, that scumbags like you
kids have even seen a—share certificate, let alone
managed to find the—money to buy any!' he yelled.

'*Mr Lancaster!* What dreadful language—I've *never*
heard anything so disgusting!' Harriet's large, grey eyes
widened in well-simulated shock and horror. Of course
she'd heard far worse swear words at the
Neighbourhood Law Centre where she worked, but

that wasn't the point, she told herself as she hastily backed away from Jake, who was by now quite clearly out of control. If Mr high-and-mighty Lancaster thought he was going to be able to intimidate her by shouting and the use of foul language, he was very much mistaken!

'Calm down, sir, we don't want any trouble, do we?' the policeman said firmly, moving adroitly to stand between the two protagonists. 'And there's no call to talk to this nice young lady like that.'

'"Nice young lady"—hah!' Jake gave a harsh bark of laughter. '*Nice* is hardly the adjective I'd use for this— this creature . . . and as for calling her "a lady" . . .?' Words seemed to fail him as he lifted his arms upward in a gesture of overwhelming frustration.

Out of the corner of her eye, Harriet saw that a television van had arrived, and that a cameraman together with a reporter holding a microphone were pushing their way through the crowd behind Jake's tense, rigid figure. Swiftly turning towards the policeman—and the camera—she tried her hardest to appear weak and frightened.

'Please . . . please don't let Mr Lancaster hit me . . .' she begged, her eyes filling with tears.

'You ought to be downright ashamed of yourself, mate!' an onlooker called out to Jake, and a responsive murmur of 'Ah . . .' and 'Shame . . .' ran round the crowd.

'Hit her?' Jake snarled. 'I wouldn't dream of it—even boiling in oil would be too kind a fate for someone who prints lies like this!' As he turned, brandishing the leaflet, his figure stiffened in shock at the realisation that he was facing a T.V. camera.

'Good afternoon,' the reporter murmured with an encouraging smile. 'It is Mr Jason Lancaster, isn't it? I wonder if we could, perhaps, just have a few words from you about this demonstration . . . hmm?'

Sobering up at the speed of light, Jake came to his senses with a sickening thud. How that damned girl had managed to out-talk, outwit and outmanoeuvre him, he had no idea, but he had no intention of further compounding any of the mistakes he had already made during their confrontation. By an enormous effort of will, he managed to compose his face, if not into a friendly smile, at least into the nearest approximation to one that he could produce at the moment.

'I'm sorry, but I'm afraid that I really can't stop,' he said firmly. 'I'm already late for an important meeting.'

It took Jake some time to force his way through the crowd, grinding his teeth in fury as he caught snatches of the interview which that quite outrageous, dreadful girl was giving the television reporter.

'. . . Miss Drummond . . . yes, I really do hold two thousand preference shares in his horrid company . . . Mr Lancaster's simply awful . . . shouting and swearing! . . . poor Mrs Elsie Peters . . . just thrown out into the street . . . modern jerry-building . . . wicked property developers . . . yes, hard and cruel—just like Simon Legree . . .!'

'*Ross!* Jake bellowed as he reached the relative sanctuary of the foyer. 'I want you to scrutinise every shareholder's pass, and if you let that girl into the meeting—you're fired!'

'But, sir, if she really is a genuine shareholder as she claims . . .?'

'I don't care what you do—hit her over the head, drug her, chloroform her . . . anything! Just as long as you make sure she doesn't manage to go through those doors.' He gestured towards the large conference hall on the ground floor. 'If she gets in—you're out! Understand?'

'Yes, sir,' Ross muttered unhappily, moving over to

the entrance and beginning to carefully look at the
passes carried by those arriving for the meeting.

Outside in the street, Harriet beamed at the reporter.
'Will you really put it out on the News tonight? Aren't
you a darling!'

The reporter's cheeks flushed and he nervously
adjusted his tie as he gazed up at the beautiful girl who
towered above him. 'How about coming out with me
for a drink tonight?' he asked hopefully.

'Oh, dear, I'd love to, but I'm afraid I can't make it,'
she said, trying to curb and disguise her impatience to
be off. 'Maybe another time, hmm?' With another
beaming smile, she blew him a kiss and hurried back to
her companions.

'Okay, let's get out of here and back to the van as
fast as possible. We haven't much time to put "Plan
Two" into operation,' Andrew warned her.

'That was really great!' said Miles, who was studying
for his doctorate in Natural Sciences. 'I've never seen
anyone quite so cross and angry before—I nearly died
laughing! Did you see his face when he read that
leaflet?'

'Well, I thought it was lucky that the policemen were
there,' Rosie said soberly as they reached the van. 'You
took a bit of a risk, Harry. Jake Lancaster seems a
thoroughly nasty piece of goods to me. I hope you and
Andrew know what you're doing?' she added, watching
anxiously as Andrew lifted a wheelchair down from the
back of the vehicle.

'No problem—we'll be fine,' Harriet assured her,
stripping off the cerise satin blouse to reveal a figure
hugging black T-shirt. Reaching inside the van for a
large shopping bag, she withdrew a smart black coat
and swiftly put it on, placing a pearl choker around her
neck and stuffing her long, wavy chestnut tresses inside
a black woollen turban, which hid all trace of her hair.

Slipping on a large pair of dark glasses, she turned to the others: 'Well, what do you think? Will I pass muster?'

'If no one sees your jeans and those hideous boots, I reckon you'll just about get by!' Rosie said with a grin. 'Where on earth did you find that ghastly turban?'

'Do you mind! It belongs to my Aunt Clarissa—which reminds me, I must get it back before she discovers it's missing.'

'Come on, Harry, stop messing about and get in the wheelchair,' Andrew said firmly.

Seating herself in the mobile chair, she looked at Andrew who was now attired in a smart black jacket over his black trousers, a neat white shirt, dark tie and chauffeur's cap completing his outfit. 'You look perfect,' she assured him as he too put on a pair of dark glasses before tucking a rug around her scarlet jeans and yellow boots. 'Have you got the passes?' she asked.

'Yes, but I wish I wasn't so sure that they're going to rumble us,' he muttered uneasily. 'And for God's sake don't let that rug slip off your knees, or we'll have had it. Oh, help—you've forgotten your gloves.'

'They're here,' Harriet pulled them out of the pocket of her coat. 'Now, don't worry, everything's going to be fine.'

Arriving back at the entrance to the building, they found themselves among a group of late arrivals. Harriet wished she felt as confident as she had tried to appear to her friends. It was clear, from the way that the commissionaire was looking at the passes carried by the shareholders, that Jake had reacted as she feared he might: there was no doubt that Harriet Drummond was definitely *persona non grata*. Trying to still the hands which had been anxiously twisting in her lap, she closed her eyes and prayed that all would go well.

Luckily, the elderly gentleman in front of them

decided to take grave exception to the unusual security
measures. Protesting that he had held shares in the
company for twenty years, and had never had to suffer
such indignity, he caused such a commotion that by the
time he had finished complaining, and it was Andrew
and Harriet's turn to be scrutinised, the commissionaire
hardly bothered with the lady in the wheelchair being
looked after by her chauffeur.

Very nearly home and dry! Harriet could feel her
excitement mounting as Andrew wheeled the chair
down the side of the conference hall, stopping beside
some chairs about seven rows back from the raised dais,
on which were seated the senior directors of Lancaster
International. Jake Lancaster was on his feet addressing
the meeting, and it was clear that he was already more
than half way through his speech.

'. . . And so you can see, ladies and gentlemen, that
our firm and its diverse companies continues to
prosper. Consolidated revenues increased to six-
hundred and fifty million dollars in the year under
review. Cash provided by the various company
operations is substantial, and we do not foresee
abnormal requirements for capital expenditure. We
have continued our policy of emphasising debt
reduction and improving productivity. At the same
time, we have developed new products and allied
services to maintain the leadership of our companies in
their worldwide markets . . .'

Blah-blah-blah! thought Harriet as the meaningless
words and figures flowed past her head. Looking up at
Jake Lancaster's tall, powerful figure, he seemed to be
perfectly relaxed as he smoothly took his shareholders
through the Annual Report. Hard was the word for
him, she decided. Hard blue eyes, hard angular cheek
bones, and a hard, firm mouth—all features that clearly
proclaimed that he would not suffer fools gladly,

neither would he stand for any interference in his life. At the moment, Jake was exuding relaxed, warm friendly charm, but she wasn't fooled—not for one minute. Standing up there was a very dangerous man, and although she told herself she wasn't frightened of him, she couldn't prevent a chill from feathering down her spine.

'. . . And therefore, ladies and gentlemen, I think we can be confident that the outlook for the coming year can only be one of optimism, and I look forward to leading this company to an even higher degree of financial success in the future. I will now hand you over to Sir Humphrey Ellis.'

There was a loud round of applause as Jake sat down, and a director stood up. 'Before I propose the resolution that the annual accounts should be approved, Mr Lancaster has indicated that he will be pleased to answer any questions from the floor.'

'Big deal!' Harriet muttered under her breath, waiting while one or two mundane matters were raised, before nudging Andrew, who responded by waving to catch the eye of the Director.

'Yes, you have a question, Sir . . . Madam . . .?'

'I was very disturbed to see outside this building, some placards maintaining that this company is insolvent,' Harriet spoke in a loud, clear voice. 'Furthermore, a leaflet handed out by the young people seemed to infer that this company was acting in an improper manner, by evicting an old lady from her home. Can Mr Lancaster enlighten his shareholders on this matter, and at the same time reassure them that no such action is contemplated?'

Jake peered through the strong lights which lit the dais. All he could see was the figure of a woman, who seemed to be seated in a wheelchair, her face hidden in the shadows at the side of the room. Surely he knew

that voice? Someone he'd met recently ...? His concentration on the problem was interrupted by Sir Humphrey indicating that the meeting was waiting for an answer.

'I have already apologised to this meeting for the unseemly demonstration, which took place earlier outside this building,' he said, rising to his feet. 'An unfortunate affair, and one that I promise will not be repeated. Young students nowadays ...' he paused and shrugged his shoulders, giving the meeting a rueful smile. 'Maybe next year, they will decide to pick on the Bank of England instead!' He sat down to a rumble of laughter.

'Answer my question, please,' Harriet demanded in a firm voice. 'You have told us that the company is not bankrupt—a statement that appears to be confirmed by the auditors who have examined your consolidated balance sheet. However, I have heard nothing about a subsidiary company, Metropolitan Development Limited, which is engaged upon wholesale development in the Caledonian Road area of London. Are they, or are they not, trying to evict old ladies to make way for their new development?'

Jake stood up. 'I must tell you, madam, that I know nothing about such an action on the part of a subsidiary company. I can only suggest that you should ignore such hysterical and emotive nonsense, especially when promulgated by wild, anarchic students.'

'If you, as Chairman and Managing Director of Lancaster International, do not know what is being done by one of your subsidiaries, Mr Lancaster,' Harriet retorted scathingly, 'then I suggest that you step down from the position you now hold, and hand over to someone who is more in touch with the affairs of this large company!'

She could see Jake's figure grow tense, his mouth

hardening into a tight line. 'You seem, if I may say so, madam, to be making a very serious allegation about the conduct of one of our companies. I have to repeat that I know nothing about the matter. However,' he added hurriedly as some of the audience began to mutter amongst themselves, 'I can assure this meeting that I will give the matter my immediate attention. If I find that any irregularities have occurred, I can promise you that they will be dealt with very promptly. Will you accept that assurance?'

'Yes, if such an assurance is entered in the minutes of this meeting,' Harriet replied. Feeling almost drunk with the success she had achieved, she was far too excited to notice Jake suddenly click his fingers in annoyance, and beckon to a young man standing at the side of the dais, whispering in his ear as Sir Humphrey Ellis proposed the adoption of the Annual Accounts.

'That went better than we could possibly have hoped,' she murmured happily as Andrew turned the wheelchair and pushed her towards the large doors which led into the foyer. 'He'll have to enter his promise into the minutes, and if we can get to a 'phone and tip off the *Evening Standard* . . .'

'Excuse me, Sir. I wonder if I could ask for some assistance?'

Harriet tried to see who it was talking to Andrew, but at that moment she felt the rug beginning to slip off her lap. Quickly tucking it firmly around her hips and legs, she heard Andrew mutter something about giving a hand with an old lady who had fainted, and that he'd be back in a minute.

Trying to suppress her annoyance at being temporarily abandoned by her fellow conspirator, she watched him hurrying after a young man through the doors to the foyer and out of sight. He'll be back soon, she assured herself, and she could hardly resent him helping

an elderly woman, since they were, after all, only in this
den of capitalism because of old Mrs Elsie Peters . . .

Her thoughts were sharply interrupted as she felt
someone seize the handles of the wheelchair, and she
found she was being propelled swiftly forward, passing
through a side door into a small hall at the rear of the
foyer.

'What's going on?' she gasped helplessly, craning her
head backwards in an effort to see the person who had
so abruptly and suddenly taken control of the
wheelchair. But try as she might, the figure was only a
dark blur at the corner of her eyes, and before she could
open her mouth to protest, she found herself being
pushed inside a small lift, the doors shutting with a hiss
and her stomach lurching as she, and whoever had
abducted her, were swept upwards.

'I don't know who you are, or what you think you
are doing,' she said as firmly as she could, addressing
the blank cream-coloured wall of the lift. 'If you don't
want to be in serious trouble, I suggest that you take me
downstairs immediately!'

The only response to her words was a faint rumble of
sardonic laughter, almost inaudible over the noise of
the machinery as they soared upwards. Just when she
thought she would begin to scream with frustration at
her extraordinary abduction, the lift halted and her
chair was jerked smartly backwards. Speeding through
what seemed to be a large reception area, and on past
various outer offices, Harriet had a confused impression
of beautifully decorated and luxurious surroundings.
Various people, mostly women, looked up from their
work to stare in astonishment as the wheelchair and its
occupant travelled past them like a high speed train.

Finally entering a very large room, she heard a door
slam shut behind her before a mighty push on one of
the handles resulted in her chair spinning like a top.

Feeling sick and dizzy, she closed her eyes until she felt the wheelchair slow down its revolutionary gyration. When she did open them again, she saw that she was facing a large desk, on the edge of which a tall man had half-seated himself, his arms crossed over his chest as he regarded her flustered, confused figure with grim, sardonic amusement.

Oh, no! *It was Jake Lancaster . . .!*

CHAPTER TWO

HARRIET looked quickly around the large room, which appeared to be Jake Lancaster's private office. Other than the door which lay behind her, there was clearly no other avenue of escape. She hadn't a hope of reaching the door and leaving the building without being caught, so she couldn't see any alternative other than to try and bluff her way out. Surely he wouldn't be rude or unkind to a supposedly crippled woman in a wheelchair? Although, looking at the steely gleam in his blue eyes, she wasn't willing to bet on it.

'My, my, that was certainly a very interesting question you raised at the meeting,' Jake Lancaster said in a slow drawl. 'Somehow, I don't know why, but I just *knew* that you'd like me to answer it more fully, hmm?'

The menace behind his softly spoken words was almost tangible in the quiet room, and it took all the courage and resolution at Harriet's command to quell the nervous, heart-thumping apprehension which seemed to have invaded her body. She could only be grateful that her trembling legs were well covered from his piercing gaze.

'That's—that's very kind of you, Mr Lancaster. However, there was really no need to—er—bring me up here. I'm—I'm quite content with your promise to look into Mrs Peter's case, and your assurance that it will be minuted.' She took a deep breath, trying to keep her voice calm and steady. 'I—I'd like to stay, of course, but—er—unfortunately I am in rather a hurry. So, if you don't mind . . .?'

'Oh, but I do! I wouldn't dream of letting you go—certainly not before we've had a good long talk. And we have so much to talk about, don't we?' He paused, lifting a dark, satanic eyebrow.

Harriet tried to think of something constructive to say, but her brains seemed to have been temporarily turned into a mass of cotton wool. If only she didn't have such a paralysingly numbing presentiment of what he was going to say next . . .

Jake gave her a grim, wolfish smile. 'Yes, I'm sure it would be very rude, not to say downright uncivil of me, if I didn't insist on continuing our discussion. I'm certain you can't have forgotten our interesting, if somewhat acrimonious argument down on the sidewalk, which was so abruptly terminated earlier this afternoon, hmm?'

Oh, God—he knows! Harriet felt a frisson of fear run through her as she realised the game was up. She could have wept with frustration at having been so near to victory, but it now looked very much as if Jake Lancaster was going to have—and enjoy—his pound of flesh. She watched helplessly as he raised himself to his full height and walked slowly towards her, bending down to whip away the rug from her knees.

'Ah, yes—Miss Drummond, I presume!' He gave a harsh bark of laughter, his cold blue eyes mocking her evident confusion. 'Well, I must say that you've had a very good run for your money, but it was your bad luck not to know that I never forget a voice. And in your case, my dear girl, once heard and seen—*never forgotten!*'

Harriet shrugged as nonchalantly as she could. 'Okay, so what happens now? Are you planning to let me go, or do you intend to call in the police?'

'Neither of those options appeals to me at the moment,' he replied smoothly. 'Why don't you get out

of that ridiculous wheelchair, while I mix us two very strong drinks? After the traumas of this afternoon, I definitely feel the need for a medicinal dose of strong liquor!'

Climbing out of the chair and stretching her cramped limbs, Harriet watched his tall figure move across the room, her heart heavy with foreboding. Jake Lancaster was taking it all far too calmly—certainly if his rage and anger out in the street had been anything to go by. For the first time that day, she took a good, hard, searching look at the man standing by the drinks cabinet.

The late afternoon sunshine pouring into the room flicked across his dark brown hair, highlighting the few threads of silver at the temples. His skin was very brown as if he spent most of his time in the open air— not the usual environment for a banker, she thought. Harriet had experienced his furious temper earlier in the day, and it didn't look as if that hard face laughed very much, if at all.

But now, as he came over to place a drink in her hand, standing before her in his well-cut dark grey lounge suit, his wide, powerful shoulders and lean hips emphasised by the immaculate formality of his clothes, she noted that his mouth was curved into a sardonic smile. It was an expression at once mocking and wicked, and she remembered Rosie's exclamation, when she had been pressed into service to help find and select a suitable photograph for the leaflet: 'Wow! Doesn't he look sexy!' Harriet had looked at her friend with amazement. To her eyes, Jake Lancaster had merely seemed to personify the archetypal image of a hard-nosed business tycoon. But now, as her senses became suddenly and sharply aware of the aggressive masculinity of the man gazing at her, she wasn't sure what she thought any longer. At such close proximity, his

strong, forceful and menacing personality seemed to be almost overpowering, and when his fingers brushed lightly against hers as he handed her a glass of whisky, she tingled as if from a slight electric shock.

'Yes,' Jake murmured reflectively, slowly sipping his drink as he conducted an appraisal of the girl standing before him, 'I must say, that's certainly some outfit you're wearing! Tell me, where do you go shopping for your clothes? Quite frankly, Miss Drummond, I don't think I can *ever* recall seeing a woman dressed quite like you before—or is it maybe the latest line in *haute couture*?'

The lazy, mocking words brought a flush of colour to her cheeks. She'd forgotten all about her crazy get-up, which together with the cerise blouse had been part and parcel of the demonstration. But now, standing here dressed like God knows what, and with the hateful man looking at her as if she was something nasty the cat had dragged in, he was succeeding in making her feel a complete and utter fool.

Calm down—and pull yourself together! she told herself, quickly suppressing an impulse to explain exactly why she was dressed the way she was. There was absolutely no reason to let Jake's sarcasm affect her. And, what was more, there was equally no reason to be feeling so apprehensive and awkward. Goodness knows, she'd met plenty of very high-powered business men, none of whom she had found to be particularly awe-inspiring.

So, let him do the talking, she thought. There was no point in her saying anything, not until she knew exactly why he'd brought her up here. And if he should start shouting, or get violent, there seemed to be plenty of people in the outer offices who would undoubtedly come to her aid if need be.

Satisfied that she had made the right, tactical

decision, Harriet put her glass down on a nearby table. Turning away from his penetrating eye, she took off her gloves and the black turban, tossing back her brilliant chestnut hair so that it fell, heavy and waving, around her shoulders. Removing the heavy black coat was a relief, the thick material being totally unsuitable for such a warm, June day. There was nothing she could do about the skin-tight scarlet jeans, nor about the hideous yellow boots which she had borrowed from a friend, but she already felt in better shape to do battle with the boss of Lancaster International.

'Stripping for action, Miss Drummond?' Jake murmured, shocking her into immobility for a moment as he uncannily echoed her thoughts. 'I don't think you will be needing these, either,' he added, reaching forward and removing her sun glasses.

Feeling absurdly naked without their dark protection, Harriet's face burned as she watched his eyes move slowly over her tall figure. The intense, insulting thoroughness with which he scrutinised her high, firm breasts and the long curving length of her legs, brought an angry sparkle to her large grey eyes. Never before had she felt such an urge to kick someone hard in the shins as she did at this moment—absolutely never!

'It's no good glaring at me like that, my girl!' His eyes flashed with sardonic amusement, and it filled her with fury to realise that he was clearly enjoying her discomfiture. 'Moreover, it seems ridiculous to keep calling you "Miss Drummond",' he continued. 'Would you like to tell me your Christian name?'

She regarded him warily for a moment, and then shrugged her shoulders. 'Not particularly, but I suppose you can call me Harriet—always providing that you don't shout, scream or use bad language.'

'And if I do? Will you tell me to go away and wash

my mouth out with soap and water?' he grinned.

'That, Mr Lancaster, is definitely the first and only sensible thing I've heard you say all day!'

Quite without thought, Harriet found herself smiling in response to the warm, amused sensuality of the low laugh with which he greeted her sharp retort. How—how extraordinary, she thought, looking at him in confusion. One minute she felt she could quite cheerfully murder him, and the next it was if she and Jake were somehow sharing a secret joke, known only to the two of them. Quickly seizing up her drink from the table, she buried her nose in the glass and tried to bring some sort of order to bear upon the chaos in her brain. She really must not allow herself to become distracted from the matter in hand—namely the fate of old Mrs Elsie Peters. And then she was struck by a sudden pang of guilt—thanks to having been abducted and whizzed up here at the speed of light, she had forgotten all about Andrew!

'Where is my friend?' she demanded.

'The boy who was pushing your wheelchair?' he asked.

'Yes—what have you done with him? If you've harmed a hair of his head, I'll have you in court so fast you won't know what's hit you!'

'You know something?' Jake murmured, his hard blue eyes gazing at her with speculation. 'I find it very interesting to note just how often you mention the law—and yet you are clearly far too young to be an attorney.'

'Am I? Well, that's hardly your affair, is it? And I'm still waiting for an answer. What have you done with Andrew?'

'You obviously possess a cool, calm and logical mind,' he mused, ignoring her question. 'Well, Harriet, if you haven't considered the law as a profession, I

recommend that you do so—I'm sure you'll be a great success.'

Patronising swine! What she did with her life was none of his damn business, although she had difficulty in suppressing an overwhelming urge to tell him that she had just taken her final law exams, and was waiting to hear the results.

As Jake's piercing blue eyes assessed her smouldering expression, he grinned with cynical amusement. 'I'm touched by your concern for your boyfriend, but he's quite all right. He was shown straight to the front door of this building, and told to go home and behave himself. Okay?'

'Yes, I suppose so,' she muttered, her words being interrupted by the ringing of the telephone.

Jake walked over to the desk and lifted the receiver, listening quietly for a moment before putting it down. He turned to look at Harriet, all trace of amusement wiped from his face which now seemed to be carved from stone, and staring at her with a deep intensity she found distinctly unnerving. It was as if he was trying to mentally bore his way into her head, swamping her with the force of his dominant personality. She quickly looked away from those all-seeing, penetrating eyes.

'Now, that is very interesting—very interesting indeed. You know something, Harriet? I would have been willing to bet my bottom dollar that there was no way a girl like you could possibly have got her hands on any shares in my company.'

'Yes,' she snapped. 'You said so earlier. If my recollection is correct, the word you used to describe me was "scumbag". I have no idea what the word means, but I can only assume you intended to be insulting. You will be pleased to hear that you succeeded!'

'There you go again—that explicit, precise use of the

English language. You really are, without doubt, the most extraordinary girl I've ever met.'

'From your exposure in the media—with one gorgeous girl after another hanging on your arm—you undoubtedly consider yourself an expert, if not a connoisseur, on the subject,' she drawled scathingly, giving way to an urgent impulse to strike back at the man regarding her as if she was an insect on the end of a pin.

'Oh, yes, indeed I do!' he agreed imperturbably. 'So, you can imagine my surprise on being informed just now that Miss Harriet Drummond, an obvious candidate for any left-wing looney party, does in fact hold two thousand preference voting shares in the company. At today's quotation of four hundred pence per share, that amounts to approximately eight thousand pounds. Now, where on earth do you suppose she found the money to buy them?'

'Maybe I go around holding up banks for a living?' she gave him a brilliant, secretive smile, that she dearly hoped would infuriate him. 'Incidentally, I'm not a "left-wing looney" as you so charmingly put it. But I'm sure such an epithet is infinitely preferable than being called, as in your case, "a bloated capitalist".'

'Ah, I see we have arrived at the sad case of Mrs Elsie Peters, have we not?' Jake murmured, picking up the leaflet from his desk.

'And about time too!' Harriet snapped. 'There is absolutely no doubt that your subsidiary company— and at least one of its directors—is acting disgracefully. Do you know what's going on? Have you seen the architect's plans? The new development is nothing but a crowded rabbit warren. Let me tell you . . .'

'That's enough!' His cold, hard voice cracked across her words like a whiplash. 'I've had about as much nonsense from you as I can stand in one day. Don't

make the grave mistake of pushing me too far, young lady. There are no policemen or T.V. reporters up here—so I suggest you watch your step, or you'll be very, *very* sorry. Do I make myself clear?'

'Okay, okay,' she muttered nervously, backing up towards the window as he moved furiously towards her. Jake's brilliant blue eyes beneath the heavy lids were radiating dire threats and dreadful consequences to anyone, such as herself, who was so foolish as to tangle with his powerful personality. Why hadn't she used a more conciliatory tone with him? She wasn't achieving anything for old Mrs Peters by taking a hard, aggressive line, and it now looked as if she'd blown it. Why, oh why had she been so stupid as to forget all she'd read about this man? She was well aware of his ruthless, meteoric rise to fame and prominence in the world of international finance. He was clearly a killer shark, and she was dismayed to find that she had somehow lost her usual self-confidence, suddenly feeling like a very small fish swimming in dangerous and uncharted waters.

'You've had a lot of fun at my expense today, Harriet,' he said with soft, terrifying menace as he halted only inches away from her trembling figure. 'And I can see you also had a lot of fun composing this leaflet. My "latest fiancée" . . .? How many fiancées am I supposed to have had, for God's sake? For your information, this is the first time I've ever been engaged to be married, okay?'

'Yes, well—I'm sorry if I got that wrong,' she mumbled, staring down at her boots.

'You are clearly a very silly young girl, who is playing games well outside her league,' he continued coldly. 'I do indeed live in a penthouse apartment, but who are you to be judge and jury about my views on this poor old lady—a woman I've never even heard about before today, hmm?'

He waited for her reply, and when none was forthcoming, he placed a finger under her chin, forcing her head up towards him. The room seemed to shrink about them, his dark and dangerous figure violently disrupting her senses. Harriet tried to look away, but her eyes remained firmly locked by the intense, searching, almost hypnotic gaze with which he seemed to be invading her very soul. The silence lengthened, the tension mounting second by second until Harriet could almost feel it hammering against her skull. How long they stood staring at each other, she had no idea, the spell being broken by the harsh sound of Jake swearing under his breath as he turned to stride quickly away across the room.

'Very well, Harriet,' he said, seating himself behind his desk. 'I suggest that you come and sit down, and that we both try to keep very, *very* calm while we review the case of Mrs Peters, hmm?'

It was some moments before Harriet could respond, finding it extraordinarily difficult to control a sudden breathlessness, and a weakness which appeared to be affecting her legs. Fighting to regain her equilibrium, she burned with resentment and a deep longing to let fly with some clever, wounding remark that would puncture the self-possession of this man who was succeeding in making her feel like a scrubby schoolgirl. However, since it seemed that Jake was prepared to discuss the burning problem of Mrs Peters, she was going to have to stifle her anger—for the moment, anyway. But, by the time she had walked over the thick carpet to a chair by his desk, aware of his hard blue eyes flicking over the black T-shirt which clung tightly to the generous curves of her high, firm breasts, she was flushed and simmering with fury.

She might well be a 'silly young girl' as he'd called her, but she, Harriet, was quite old enough to know

when a man was mentally undressing her—and she didn't find it at all amusing. Promising herself that however long it took, she would somehow get even with the foul man, she sat down, striving to clear her mind of all vengeful thoughts and concentrate on the matter of old Elsie Peters.

'Now,' Jake said, glancing down at the leaflet. 'I note that you are claiming that this lady's house is about to be demolished, to make way for new development—not an unusual occurrence, I think you will agree. However, I'm prepared to give you ten minutes of my valuable time in which to explain exactly why you consider this matter to be so important.'

'And if I possessed double the amount of shares than I do, would I be permitted twenty minutes of your "valuable time" . . .?' Harriet's voice was heavy with sarcasm.

Jake's mouth tightened and he pushed a hand roughly through his thick dark hair. 'I wish to God I knew why I'm even bothering to listen to you at all! You've already forced me to lose my temper once today, and I'm very near to doing so again,' he growled. 'If you know what's good for you, I suggest you get the hell out of here—right this minute!'

They glared at each other across the desk for a few moments, before Harriet's common sense slowly reasserted itself.

'You may not believe me, but I wasn't trying to be deliberately irritating—or at least, not entirely,' she added honestly. 'I was, in fact, making a valid point, because it isn't just a case of one old lady losing her home. There are a lot of factors involved with the redevelopment area that I'm almost sure you don't know about, and I'm going to need more than ten minutes to explain all the ramifications.'

Jake sighed and leaned back in his chair. 'Forget I

mentioned that you should become a lawyer, Harriet. God knows, you have all the persistence and sheer, damn nerve to make a top-selling insurance agent! I have a hollow feeling that I am *definitely* going to regret this,' he added wearily, 'but okay, start talking.'

Harriet paused for a moment to collect her thoughts. This was the only opportunity she was going to have to plead Mrs Peters' case, and she must get it right. Jake Lancaster was clearly no fool, and she could see little point in appealing to his finer, humanitarian feelings. Not only was she convinced he didn't have any moral values worth a damn, but even if he did, they were likely to lag far behind his commercial instincts. Profit and loss—and maybe not wanting to be publicly branded as a wicked property developer—those were the points on which she must lay the heaviest emphasis.

'I have no way of knowing just how involved you are. in the day to day business of one of your subsidiary companies. So, possibly I should confine myself to the bare bones of the situation.' She waited to see if he had any comment to make, but he merely nodded his dark head and indicated that she should continue.

Taking a deep breath, Harriet began to calmly and logically relate the story of how one of his companies, Metropolitan Development, had bought a considerable amount of land from the Church Commissioners. On this land were several old, disused factories, two streets of leasehold houses in bad condition and a large piece of derelict land, at present used as a scrap metal yard. The first plan submitted to the local council had not been approved, but when the company applied to the council again, with another plan which doubled the amount of houses, they were successful in gaining permission.

'The only snag, for the company, was that more houses equalled more people,' Harriet explained. 'To

gain a proper exit from the site, they had to include a small street of some fifteen houses, all in private ownership. None of those owners—among whom is Mrs Elsie Peters—want to sell their houses to the Metropolitan Development Company. Some of the people in that street have lived there all their lives, they see no reason why they should move, and . . .'

'Just a minute,' Jake frowned, looking up from the notes he had been making. 'As I understand it, the first plan was turned down, but the second plan, with vastly increased density of housing, was approved. Why?'

'That's exactly the question I asked myself,' Harriet grinned. 'You see, when Mrs Peters first came to see us, I didn't know anything about the plans. I felt sorry for the old woman, but it sounded like so many of the cases we get, and I didn't really see what I could do for her.'

'Who are "we" and "us"?' he queried.

Harriet hesitated for a moment, and then shrugged her shoulders. 'I work part-time in a Neighbourhood Law Centre, where we provide free legal advice for those people who can't afford to pay solicitors' fees.'

'Ah . . .!' Jake's mouth twitched with wry amusement. 'It's nice to know that I was right. So you are a lawyer, after all!'

'No, not yet. I'm waiting for the result of my final law exams.'

'I have no doubt that you will pass with flying colours,' he said drily. 'However, I am intrigued to know more about why the local council changed their mind about granting planning permission.'

'I'm not sure that you will want to know, but the simple answer is: graft and corruption! One of the directors of Metropolitan Developments, Mr Alan Matthews, has a small, fluffy blonde wife with very expensive tastes. Her brother just happens to be the Chairman of the Planning Committee on the local

council. She, her brother and her husband have formed a small, private building company—about which I am very sure you know nothing! That small building company has been awarded the contract by Metropolitan Developments to build the houses on the new estate, some of which are being given to the local council to house those on the long waiting list.'

'My God!' Jake looked at her blankly for a moment. 'Are you absolutely certain of your facts?'

'Oh yes. Although whether they can be proved in a court of law is another matter. However, you must admit it's a neat little piece of skullduggery!' Harriet's mouth curved into a wide, cynical grin.

'If you're right, I'd call it something a lot worse,' he retorted, rising to his feet and pacing about the room.

'Well, I rather thought that the newspapers would enjoy the story,' she murmured, carefully avoiding his eyes. 'Firstly, about the family connection between the Chairman of the Planning Committee and *your* development company; and secondly, exactly how *your* development company got the go ahead, and now looks set to make lots of lovely money. Then, about how one of *your* directors, his wife and her brother, the Chairman of the Planning Committee, are all set to secretly make themselves a fortune on building the houses—you should see the plans, they're simply awful!'

Harriet turned to look up at his tall figure, trying to gauge his reaction to what she had been saying. But the tight, blank expression on his hard face was giving nothing away.

'As for the council,' she continued. 'Well, they are only too pleased that instead of having to make a capital investment in building some new houses, they can now allocate a proportion of these new homes to people on the waiting list. In fact, everyone's happy— except poor Mrs Peters and her neighbours, of course.

They don't want to sell their houses, but how can they stand up against both the development company *and* the local council who, pushed hard by—yes, you've guessed, the Chairman of the Planning Committee!—are making a compulsory purchase order.'

Absorbed in thought, Jake continued to prowl about his office before he asked, 'How come, if you think you've got such a good case, that you didn't go straight to the newspapers in the first place?'

'Believe me—we thought about it!' Harriet assured him grimly. 'But we realised that we would be making very serious accusations, upon which your company could well have tried to sue us for libel, or slapped an injunction on both of us and the newspaper. That would have made the matter *sub judice*, and would have meant that no one could talk or print comment about the new plans, until the matter came to court. By that time it would be far too late to help Mrs Peters. The demo outside your office this afternoon was just a bit of fun—window dressing, if you like—the real aim was to get the matter of your development company and its activities into your Annual Report—in which we succeeded!'

'So that if it came to court . . .'

'You'd find yourself hung, drawn and quartered!'

Jake gritted his teeth. 'Even from our brief acquaintanceship, I don't need anyone to tell me that was your *own* sweet little idea!'

'Yes, it was, actually.' Harriet grinned complacently up at him, the smile dying on her lips as she saw that he was definitely not amused. Once more, as earlier in the day, it seemed as if he was going to explode with suppressed rage, and she was relieved to hear a knock on the door.

'I know you didn't want to be disturbed, Mr

Lancaster,' his secretary murmured. 'But there's an urgent telex from Hong Kong, and . . .'

'Not now, Ann, for God's sake!' he barked. 'And I'd like two cups of strong coffee, immediately!'

'Yes, yes of course,' she muttered and withdrew, to return a few minutes later with a tray.

'Are you always so foul to your staff?' Harriet asked, as his secretary softly closed the door of the office.

'What on earth are you talking about?'

Taking her time, Harriet enjoyed a few sips of the hot liquid before putting down her cup and smiling brightly up at the man towering over her seated figure. 'It's obvious that the poor woman is terrified of you. And I'm not surprised, if that's the way you normally speak to her. Quite frankly, I wouldn't put up with your rudeness for longer than five minutes!'

'What absolute nonsense!' Jake put his cup down on the desk with a bang. 'Miss Norris is highly efficient, and I value her accordingly.'

'Oh, yes . . .?' Harriet sniffed in disbelief. 'Well, if I were you, I'd start trying to be a little more polite in future, otherwise you'll arrive one day to find that she's gone to work for a more considerate employer.'

'My God! You are absolutely incredible!' Jake's face flushed with fury as he stood glaring down at her. 'You cause a commotion outside in the street, then you try and upset the Annual General Meeting, and now you're trying to lecture me on the running of my office! Anything else you'd like to say while you're at it, Miss Drummond?'

'No, I don't think so. Not at the moment, anyway,' she murmured, pushing back her chair and rising to her feet.

'That's very wise of you,' he grated harshly, his hard blue eyes flashing with anger.

Glancing through her eyelashes at his tense, rigid

figure, Harriet swiftly decided that while it clearly wouldn't do him any harm to be told a few home truths, it might also be a good idea if she left the room as quickly as possible.

'Um ... I think that it's time I went home. I'm assuming that you will look into Mrs Peters' case, and deal with the Metropolitan Development Company ...?'

'Your assumption is quite correct,' Jake said grimly, watching as she went over to collect the clothes she had worn to the meeting. 'How are you going to get home? You can't walk the streets dressed like that!'

'It's no problem, I'll just get a taxi,' she assured him blithely.

'As far as I am aware, London taxis expect to be paid. And it would appear that you do not possess a purse. Or do you have some money hidden away in that pair of very tight jeans, hmm?' he added with sardonic mockery.

If there's one man I really hate, it's Jake Lancaster! Harriet told herself bitterly as she realised her predicament. Her handbag, containing her purse, was still in the van, where she had left it before the demonstration.

'There's no problem,' she muttered. 'If you'd just be kind enough to lend me some money ...?'

Jake didn't say anything, merely caming over to take her arm and leading her out of the office. 'I won't be long, Ann,' he called over his shoulder as he propelled Harriet swiftly towards the open door of the elevator.

'There's no need for you to come downstairs with me,' Harriet snapped, feeling uncomfortable at his close proximity, and the fact that his hand was still firmly gripping her arm.

'Oh, yes there is!' he gave a low, wry laugh. 'If I don't see you off the premises, how will I know that you've

really left? Believe me, Harriet, I can't face the thought that you might suddenly pop up like a jack-in-the-box, just when I and my directors are sitting down to a quiet meeting. I must be getting old, but I don't think my nerves can stand it!'

'Well, you shouldn't own crooked companies!' she retorted as the lift came to a halt and she found that they were in an underground car park. 'What do you think you're doing?' she demanded as he marched her over to a long, low black sports car. 'I'm not getting into that!' she cried trying to twist away from his grip.

'I am merely going to take you home,' Jake muttered, wrestling with her tall figure as she tried to hit him with the heavy black wool coat. 'Now, stop this nonsense, *at once!*' he added sharply, his arms closing about her body and pinning her firmly to his hard chest.

Gasping for breath, Harriet stared at the face only inches away from her own, at the hard, angry blue eyes glinting in the dim underground light. As they stood locked together in a strange silence amidst the distant rumble of the city traffic, the expression in his eyes seemed to change. Growing cloudy and opaque, they conveyed a message she didn't understand, but which triggered a sub-conscious response deep in her body. Through her thin T-shirt she could feel the way his heart was pounding, echoing her own wild pulse beats, and the sharp astringent aroma of his after-shave teased her nostrils. The strong arms about her tightened as his face came nearer—so close that she could see every pore, every indentation of his tanned skin—his mouth moving with infinite slowness towards her trembling lips. Good heavens—he was going to kiss her!

Thinking about it afterwards, and trying to rationalise her quite extraordinary behaviour, Harriet was at a complete loss to account for what happened next. Surely she should have screamed, or shouted, or fought

her way out of his embrace? But it seemed as if she had become mentally paralysed, her lips parting in a soft, instinctive invitation, oblivious to everything except the fierce excitement which scorched through her body as his firm mouth possessed hers.

It was only the nearby sound of a car door banging and the roar of an engine, that brought her back to her senses and she found the strength to push him away.

With legs that felt like jelly, Harriet stumbled over and leant against the car as she tried to regain her composure. Cautiously peeking through her eyelashes at Jake, she found that he was staring at her as if he had seen a ghost, his face pale beneath the tan. He didn't say anything as he came over to open the passenger door and, just as silently, she got into the car.

What could she possibly say? she thought as the sports car snaked through the narrow city streets some minutes later. Neither of them had yet said a word, and the silence seemed to hang heavily in the confined space. Glancing at the stern, handsome profile of the man beside her, Harriet turned to stare out of the side window. What had happened back in the car park seemed totally unreal. She disliked Jake and everything he stood for, and he had made it abundantly clear that he loathed her. So, what on earth had they been doing, kissing each other like that . . .?

Totally bemused by her own behaviour, let alone his, she gave a heavy sigh of bewilderment, which caused him to cast a quick, sideways glance at her silent figure.

'If you will just tell me where you live, I will get you home as quickly as I can,' he said in a harsh, grating voice. 'As for what happened just now, I suggest that we both forget it, especially since there is no likelihood of us ever having to meet each other again.'

'I had already forgotten the unfortunate episode,' Harriet retorted quickly, wondering why she was

suddenly feeling so depressed. It must be because it had been a long day, she decided. If she needed confirmation of her tired state of mind, it came when she nearly gave him directions to the house in Eaton Square. Collecting herself in the nick of time, she directed him towards the large, rather decrepit house in a dingy road behind King's Cross Station.

'Are you sure you want me to drop you here?' he asked doubtfully as he drew the vehicle up to a halt. 'It doesn't look very ... Oh, my God! Is that what I think it is?'

Harriet grinned as she followed his eyes, and saw that he was gazing in horror at the bright neon sign advertising a 'massage parlour', situated on the ground floor of the house next to hers.

'Tim and Geoffrey, who work there, are my dearest friends,' she said primly.

He looked at her, his face rigid with shock. 'You aren't going to tell me ... I mean, a girl like you, living in a place like *that* ...!'

'Don't be such a snob, Jake!' she laughed. 'However, I will relieve your worst fears by telling you that no, I don't. I live next door, okay?'

'For heaven's sake, Harriet, of course it's not okay. This is a terrible place to live,' he frowned. 'How can your parents let you stay here?'

'Both my parents were killed in a plane crash when I was twelve,' she said quietly, oddly touched by his concern. 'However, I can promise you that I live very comfortably here with my friends—not to mention Fred, Clarice and Montmorency!'

Jake sighed, and shook his head before getting out of the car and coming around to open her door. 'Look,' he said as she turned away to enter the house, 'I don't like to think that ... I mean, if you should need a square meal any time ...' he hesitated, his cheeks reddening as

she threw back her head and gave a sudden peal of laughter.

'Oh, Jake! Only half an hour ago, I was Public Enemy Number One—well, as far as you're concerned, anyway. So, how come you're now suddenly so solicitous for my welfare, and worrying about whether I've got more than a dried crust in the larder?' she asked, her shoulders shaking with amusement at the ridiculous irony of the situation in which she found herself. 'Don't tell me that the well-known, hard-nosed businessman, Jake Lancaster, is going soft on me—I can't bear it! Can it be that you have forgotten I own two thousand shares in your company?'

'No, I damn well haven't forgotten!' Jake snarled. 'And let me tell you, Harriet Drummond, that you are without doubt quite the most crazy, irritating girl I have ever had the misfortune to meet!' he shouted angrily over his shoulder as he marched back to his car. Clamping on his seat-belt, he had just started the engine when she leant down to knock on the glass window. 'For God's sake—now what do you want?'

'Not a lot,' she grinned. 'I just wanted to tell you that you've got a week to do something about Mrs Peters. If you haven't sorted it out by then, I shall be forced to contact you again. And you know *just* how much you'd hate me to do that!'

'God give me strength!' he muttered, closing his eyes for a moment, and clearly struggling for self-control. 'I give you my solemn promise that I will have the matter sorted out as soon as possible. And yes, you are quite right,' he added through clenched teeth. 'I never want to see you again—absolutely and definitely *never*!'

Jake's final words were still resounding in her ears as he let in the clutch, and his car roared away down the street.

CHAPTER THREE

'HEY, is that you, Harry?' Andrew called, bounding down the stairs as she entered the house. 'What happened to you? Are you all right? We've all been so worried—you've no idea!'

'I'm fine, really I am,' she assured him. 'I'll tell you all about it in a moment, but there's a slight problem, I'm afraid.'

'Oh, Lord! I knew I should have tried to force my way back into the building, but . . .'

'No, nothing like that,' she smiled. 'The small problem is that I left my handbag in the van. And without it, and the keys it contains, I can't get into my flat.'

'There's no problem,' he said, running upstairs and returning with her handbag a few moments later. 'Rosie found it when we took the van back, and gave it to me for safe-keeping.'

'Thanks,' Harriet said, opening the door of her ground floor flat. 'I wasn't too worried about myself, but I knew Montmorency would be hungry by now. Could you be a dear and let him in, while I dump this coat in the bedroom?'

'Sure, and I'll put the kettle on. You look as if you can do with a strong cup of tea,' Andrew said, walking across the main room and sliding open the large glass doors which led into a pretty, paved courtyard. Hardly had he slid one door open, when a large hairy grey and white dog galloped through, barking excitedly for a while before charging into Harriet's bedroom and leaping on to her bed.

'Oh, for goodness sake, get off at once you horrid boy!' she told the Old English Sheepdog, who merely gazed worshipfully up at her through his long mane of shaggy hair, panting with delight at her return. 'One word from me, and he does just as he likes!' she said ruefully as she joined Andrew in the kitchen, the dog following closely at her heels.

'Now, sit down and tell all!' he said firmly, putting the tea pot on the table beside the mugs he had found in a cupboard. 'Old Montmorency may be hungry, but he'll have to wait until I've heard what happened to you after I got thrown out of the building.'

'Quite honestly, I thought I was going to die of fright!' she laughed. 'One moment I was sitting in the wheelchair, and the next I was being whizzed up to Jake Lancaster's suite of offices ... oh, my goodness,' she frowned suddenly. 'I'd completely forgotten about the wheelchair! How on earth are we going to get that back to Geoffrey at the massage parlour? He only borrowed it from his grandfather on the strict understanding that we returned it tonight.'

'Harry!' Andrew groaned. 'Forget the wheelchair for a moment, and tell me what happened to you this afternoon—or do I have to choke it out of you!'

'Okay, okay. Calm down!' she grinned, giving the dog a biscuit before sitting down and pouring them both a mug of tea. 'Well, the good news is that it looks as if we're going to be able to help Mrs Peters,' she said, relating all that had happened to her after Andrew had been led away from her side at the close of Lancaster International's Annual General Meeting.

Well, not quite all, of course. There didn't seem any point in dwelling upon her strangely confused, see-sawing of emotions during the interview with Jake, and she certainly had no intention of telling Andrew—or anyone else, for that matter—about that extraordinary

episode in the underground car park. It wasn't just the fact that Jake had kissed her—inexplicable as his action was—it was her own, apparently quite willing response that was so baffling . . .

'That's really good news, Harry—absolutely marvellous!' Andrew's voice broke into her distracted thoughts. 'How about coming out tonight for a celebration? I said I'd meet the others in the pub at about eight o'clock, so we could go and have a pizza before we join them.'

'Oh, Andrew, I'm sorry. I can't make it tonight, I'm afraid.' Harriet glanced down at her watch. 'In fact, if I don't get a move on, I'm going to be late.'

'Who is it this time?' he demanded. 'You're hardly ever here at weekends, and you're always slipping off, never telling anyone where you're going or where you've been.'

Harriet blinked, her grey eyes widening in astonishment. When she'd bought the house next to the massage parlour, turning it into reasonably priced bed-sitting rooms for rental to impecunious students, Andrew had been almost the first to apply for a room. They had been friends now for two years, so why was he suddenly becoming so—well, so possessive?

'It's no good looking at me like that, Harry!' he said roughly, reaching forward to clasp her hand. 'You must know that I'm crazy about you. Surely you can understand why I want to know where you're going? Is it another man?'

'For goodness sake, don't be so silly,' she muttered, trying to withdraw her hand from his grasp.

'What's so silly about being madly in love with you?' Andrew jumped up from the table and began striding agitatedly about the small room. 'I know it's hopeless, but I had to say something, I . . .'

'Who's a silly boy, then . . .?' a deep voice croaked

from the top of a cupboard, followed by a piercing wolf-whistle. 'Who's a silly-billy . . .?'

'Oh—shut up, Fred!' Andrew shouted. 'Honestly, Harry, I'll throttle that damn parrot of yours one of these days! Oh Lord—are you all right?' he asked, quickly coming over to put an arm about her shaking body, and groaning with remorse as she raised her face and he saw that her eyes were full of tears. 'I'm sorry, I didn't mean to make you cry, it's just . . .'

'I'm not crying,' she gasped, wiping the moisture from her eyes as she began giggling again. 'It's just you, and Fred—it's so funny!'

'Funny? I'll show you that I'm not joking . . .' he cried hoarsely, urgently pulling her to her feet and clasping her tall figure in his arms as he began to rain kisses down on her face.

'For goodness sake—stop it, Andrew,' she said, wriggling out of his embrace, and backing away towards the living room. 'This is just—well, it's no good. I'm very fond of you, really I am,' she assured him. 'But only as a good friend. I—I'm sorry . . .' she shrugged helplessly.

'Okay, so who is he?'

'I don't know what you're talking about?'

'Who's the man you're in love with, the man you're seeing tonight?'

Harriet looked at him in bewilderment. 'The man I'm in love with . . .? You must be out of your mind! I'm not in love with anyone, for heaven's sake.' And then, when it was clear from his stony face that he didn't believe her, she gave a heavy sigh. 'If you want to know the absolute truth, I'm having to go out with my uncle, tonight. He's a member of one of the City Guilds, and they are having their annual dinner in the Mansion House. My aunt has broken her ankle and has asked me to take her place. I don't want to go. I'll be bored to

death, but I'm fond of them both and so I agreed to accompany my uncle. Satisfied?'

'Yes, I . . .' Andrew looked at her with a crestfallen expression. 'I'm sorry, I don't know what came over me just now.'

'Please, let's just forget it. We've been such good friends for a long time, and I'd hate us to fall out with each other. I'm truly sorry that I don't feel the same way you do.'

'That's okay, Harry. It's just a bit of June madness on my part, I expect,' he said sadly, going towards the door. 'Ignore what happened just now, hmm?'

'Of course I will—and we're still good friends?' she asked anxiously.

'Sure, why ever not?' He gave her a wry, crooked grin before leaving the room.

But as Harriet drove her small car towards South Kensington, she had a depressed, hollow feeling that her friendly relationship with Andrew wasn't ever going to be the same again. She'd never really been 'in love'. Infatuated with some boyfriends, maybe, but not in love. Certainly not the sort of overwhelming, earth-shaking emotion that she'd read about in books and poetry. Possibly she was one of those people who wasn't capable of deep passion? She hadn't felt anything other than a slight irritation when Andrew had clasped her in his arms. Definitely nothing at all akin to the way the blood had pounded through her body when Jake had kissed her . . . Her face flamed with colour, and resolutely banishing such erroneous thoughts from her mind, she made a determined effort to concentrate on the road in front of her.

Arriving outside the large, white stone building, she quietly let herself into the house and was about to mount the wide curving staircase, when she heard her aunt call out.

'Is that you, Harriet?'

Suppressing a sigh, she retraced her steps and entered the large drawing room where her aunt was lying on a sofa, her ankle bound in plaster.

'Ah, there you are! I was getting quite worried that you wouldn't turn up,' her aunt said petulantly. 'And why you are wearing those *dreadful* clothes, I've no idea. Don't you care what you look like? If I've said it once, I've said it a hundred times, your dear mother would turn in her grave if she could see you now. God knows, Ralph and I have done our best . . .'

Harriet continued to stand in the doorway, smiling vaguely as her Aunt Clarissa's words flowed over her head. It was a typical complaint, monotonously reiterated every time Lady Clarissa set eyes on the tall girl who so resolutely refused to conform to the wealth and position to which she had been born. Harriet had often asked herself why she put up with it, but she knew that, despite the constant moaning, her aunt was genuinely fond of her difficult niece and in a perpetual state of worry that she would marry one of the disreputable characters with whom she mixed. The thought of Harriet's money being removed from the family, and bestowed upon a charming n'er-do-well or fortune-hunter, was a possibility that caused her many sleepless nights.

'. . . Caroline's come up from Dorset for a few days. Why don't you go with her to Harrods and let her help you chose some nice frocks? You could be such a pretty girl, if only you made the effort, dear.'

'Carrie's here? Why didn't you tell me she was coming? I must dash and get changed . . .' Harriet called over her shoulder as she ran from the room, leaving her aunt sighing heavily before picking up the society magazine she had been reading when her niece had entered the house.

'Hello, stranger! What's brought you up to this neck of the woods?' Harriet smiled at her old schoolfriend who was busy unpacking her suitcase. 'I'm dying to catch up on your news, so do come and talk to me while I'm getting dressed for Uncle Ralph's shindig,' she continued, leading the way towards her own suite of rooms.

'My God! Your clothes get worse and worse!' Caroline grinned as Harriet sat down on the bed to pull off the yellow boots. 'I bet your aunt would have a fit if she could see you now.'

'She just did—and you are supposed to be taking me to Harrods "for a nice, pretty frock",' she mouthed in a close approximation to her aunt's voice. 'Actually, even I think I look dreadful, but this get-up was donned in a good cause.'

'You and your good causes! Tell me honestly, Harry, do you really like living in that awful area behind King's Cross? I'll grant that you've made your flat very attractive, but why not stay here where you can be so . . .'

'Comfortable? Pampered? Cosseted?' Harriet enquired with a laugh. 'Look, we've had this out before, haven't we? I mean, I love my aunt, but she's your mother-in-law too, and would you really want to live with her if you were me?'

'I'm quite fond of the old girl—but no, I wouldn't,' Caroline agreed. 'I'm only up here for a few days because . . .' she hesitated for a moment. 'Well, the fact is, I'm pregnant again, Harry, and Piers is insisting that I have a professional going over by the quacks in Harley Street.'

Although the words were said lightly, Harriet knew just how important this new pregnancy was for her cousin. Caroline had miscarried a baby two years ago, and had become increasingly worried when she had failed to conceive another.

'Oh darling, I'm so thrilled for you both,' Harriet said, jumping up and giving the other girl a hug. Her aunt and uncle had hoped that their son, Piers, would marry Harriet: 'so neat and tidy, dear'. But they had grown up together like an older brother and sister, and were both supremely disinterested in the idea. So Harriet had been more than delighted when Piers had met her old schoolfriend, Carrie, and had promptly fallen head over heels in love with her.

'You must absolutely and solemnly promise that I can be a godmother,' Harriet's voice was muffled as she stripped off the black T-shirt, before wriggling out of the tight scarlet jeans. 'Piers must be thrilled to bits.'

'Yes, he is—well, we both are, of course. Still, it seems a bit unlucky to be too hopeful at the moment. I'll feel safer when I've got past the first three months. Now, that's enough about me, how's life going with you these days? Met any dishy men I ought to know about?'

'You and Aunt Clarissa have a lot more in common than you realise!' Harriet grinned. 'Quite honestly, I'm far too busy helping out in the local Neighbourhood Law Centre to have time for any men—dishy or otherwise.

'Do you enjoy the work, Harry? I'd have thought some of the cases are awfully grim.'

'Well, yes, I suppose a lot of them are. Of course, I'm not qualified yet, and I've got two years of pupillage to go before I'm a fully fledged solicitor, but at least I feel I'm doing something.

'What are you going to do when you aren't technically a student anymore?' Caroline probed. 'Do you really want to keep living in that awful area of London? I take it that Aunt Clarissa doesn't know about the "dear boys" in the massage parlour next door?'

'Good God no! I've taken good care to see that she's

never been near the house. She's only got my 'phone number, not the address—I'm not a complete idiot, you know!' Harriet laughed, swiftly removing her bra and pants before walking through into her bathroom and turning on the shower. She returned, wrapped in a large bath towel, to find Caroline sitting on the bed, deep in thought.

'Look, now you've no need to live near the law school, why not buy yourself a nice house. It doesn't have to be in Knightsbridge or South Ken, Harry. There are lots of super places you could live—down by the river at Putney or Chiswick, for instance. Or north of London, in Hampstead or Highgate.'

Harried sighed. 'Of course I've thought of that. And if it was up to me, I'd really like to live in the country. You know, find a nice old fashioned firm of solicitors in a small market town, and then I could live in a pretty cottage and keep lots of animals. As you know, I find animals a lot easier to deal with than humans!' she added with a crooked smile.

'However, it's a stupid pipe-dream, of course, because what would I do about Aunt Clarissa and Uncle Ralph? You know the terms of my parent's will and the trust, as well as I do. It probably wouldn't matter to Uncle Ralph, who practically lives in his club, but Aunt Clarissa loves this huge house and, to be quite honest, the lifestyle that goes with it. With their small income, they couldn't manage to live here in London, and it would probably mean they'd have to move down to Dorset and live with you and Piers. Quite apart from how you'd feel having them underfoot, they would be miserable without all their friends.' She shrugged helplessly. 'Honestly, Carrie, the whole idea is a non-starter.'

Her friend gave a reluctant nod. Her mother and father-in-law never referred to the matter, but everyone

in the family knew that the large, imposing house in
Eaton Square had been bought by Harriet's trustees
when she had been left an orphan at the age of twelve.
Her father, John Drummond, had been a powerful and
wealthy man with multifarious world-wide investments.
His millions were held in trust until Harriet married or
reached the age of twenty-five. Until that time, his will
had stipulated that his trustees should buy a large house
for his daughter and her guardians: his wife's brother,
Sir Ralph Worthington and his wife Clarissa. If, at any
time, his daughter should cease to live in the house, it
was to be sold and the capital sum transferred to the
millions already being administered by his trustees.

Caroline felt sorry for Harriet, but she could
appreciate the problem. The trustees had accepted the
necessity for her friend to live elsewhere during the
week, nearer her law school, and had advanced the
money for her to purchase the house in that appalling
street. But they had told her that they would take quite
a different view if she moved permanently away from
the house in Eaton Square. To put it quite simply, her
aunt and uncle were totally dependent on their niece for
both the roof over their heads, and the many servants
who administered to their needs. And knowing Harriet
as she did, Caroline realised her friend had far too soft
a heart to wish to disrupt their comfortable life.

'Cheer up, Carrie! I'm the one who should be looking
miserable at having to stay chained to this damn big
house. So, why you're looking like a wet weekend, I've
no idea. Come on, help me to choose something to wear
for this boring dinner tonight.'

Looking at Harriet as she clipped on a pair of
emerald and diamond earrings left to her by her
mother, Caroline couldn't help smiling at the trans-
formation. Gone was the tall student dressed in scruffy
clothes with a long mane of hair flowing wildly about

her shoulders. In her place was a statuesque, sophisticated woman clothed in a long emerald-green chiffon evening dress, the delicate material clinging to her willowy figure and emphasising her soft curves. With her brilliant chestnut hair coiled into a smooth chignon at the nape of her neck, Harriet looked magnificent, and almost unrecognisable.

When Caroline voiced her thoughts, Harriet responded with a hoot of laughter. 'You're nuts! Thank God I don't have to dress up like this very often. Do you remember Mary-Louise, that spotty girl in the sixth form? Well, I must admit she's looking a lot better than she used to, but the poor girl has married some rich and important guy, for whom she has to throw glamorous parties morning, noon and night. I can't imagine a more ghastly fate!'

'Speaking as someone who lives on a farm in deepest Dorset, I can think of worse ways to spend one's time,' her friend retorted drily. 'And when you fall in love and get married, you'll undoubtedly be amazed to find that you'll want to please your husband, even if it means having "glamorous parties" every now and then! Besides,' she added with a grin, 'don't tell me that you'd always want to live in your squalid road. Surely you enjoy coming back here to be spoiled rotten? I know I would!'

Harriet found herself pondering Caroline's final words as she sat beside her uncle in the back of the chauffeur-driven vintage Rolls Royce. She often used to laugh at the ancient Rolls, one of the great loves of Sir Ralph's life—the other being his club in St James Street. But she had to admit that there were occasions, such as tonight when she was wearing a dress she didn't want crushed, that she was grateful for its huge size and comfort. As Simmons, the chauffeur, drove through the now deserted streets of the City, Harriet was honest

enough to acknowledge that life in her ground floor flat
left much to be desired. Especially when she was trying
to study, and the student in the room above insisted on
playing his stereo at full pitch. It was at such moments
that she was glad to be able to escape back to the peace
and quiet of the large house. But only as an occasional
refuge.

She had been desperately lonely there as a child, only
seeing Piers when he was home in the holidays. She had
longed to be allowed to follow his example and go away
to boarding school, but her guardians and the trustees
wouldn't hear of it. She had to go to a day school in
London, and her aunt and uncle actively discouraged
her from bringing back home any of the friends she had
made there. In fact, the only times she had been totally
and completely happy had been the long summer
holidays spent on the Worthingtons' run-down family
estate in Dorset.

Following her uncle Ralph up the stairs and through
the magnificent reception rooms of the Mansion House,
Harriet tried to make interesting conversation with
some of the people to whom she was introduced.
However, most of the talk was about City affairs and
growing bored, she gazed idly around the room. It was
a formal banquet, and the men were dressed in white tie
and tails. On tall, slim men the old fashioned evening
wear looked fine, but many of the city figures present
were short and rotund, and Harriet thought that they
resembled nothing more than a crowd of small, fat
penguins. She was smiling at the idea when she
suddenly stiffened, blinking her eyes with incredulity. It
couldn't be? Surely not? But as she heard the names
sonorously announced, she realised with a sinking
feeling that her eyes hadn't deceived her.

There, walking slowly down the receiving line, and
shaking hands with the Master and Junior Wardens of

the Worshipful Company of Foresters was Jake Lancaster! Bending her knees and trying to hide behind her uncle, Harriet's brain whirled as she tried to think what she was going to do. The reception room was filling up and so there was a possibility, if she was very careful, that she could avoid Jake seeing her. It would certainly be disastrous for all sorts of reasons if he did. Quite apart from the fact that not even Andrew and her student friends knew of her rich background— something she had taken infinite pains to conceal— there was Uncle Ralph to consider. If he thought about it at all, she was sure he imagined her to be pursuing her studies in a quiet hostel or lodging. One word from Jake about the massage parlour, for instance, and the fat would really be in the fire! She might be able to twist her uncle round her little finger, but Aunt Clarissa was another matter entirely. To get Harriet away from such insalubrious surroundings, her aunt was quite capable of calling in the aid of her trustees, and Harriet knew they would be shocked and horrified to learn exactly where she was living.

And there was the matter of Jake himself. Not only had he been furious when he'd left her earlier in the afternoon, but as far as he was aware, she was just a young student who had caused him a certain amount of trouble. She wasn't entirely sure how he would react when he discovered who she was, but she had no illusions about the fact that he would at least be very angry. It didn't look to her as if Jake Lancaster would take kindly to being fooled, even by such a small fish as Harriet.

Feverishly searching through the booklet containing the menu and a seating plan, which every guest had been handed on their arrival, Harriet gave a sigh of relief to find that Jake wasn't apparently seated anywhere near her position. In fact, she couldn't see his

name at all, and it was only when her eyes fell on the
list of speakers, that she realised he was one of the
guests of honour.

Her uncle turned to introduce her to a newcomer,
and in doing so, gave her a clear and uninterrupted
view of Jake and his fiancée standing across the far side
of the room.

There was no doubt that the formal male evening
attire suited Jake down to the ground. His tall, dark
handsome figure looked sensationally attractive in the
garments which were so seldom worn nowadays. Her
gaze swept over the stiff white shirt, white waistcoat
and bow tie, contrasting so sharply against his deeply
tanned skin, and the black-tailed coat, cut short in front
at the waist and which emphasised his wide, powerful
shoulders. He looked what he clearly was: a magnificent
male specimen. Her friend Rosie had been right all
along! Harriet thought, suddenly realising that the deep
throbbing excitement in the pit of her stomach was the
strong, primeval force of sexual attraction. Feeling
momentarily quite faint, she realised that not to put too
fine a point upon it, Jake Lancaster was, in Rosie's
immortal words . . . 'a very sexy gent!'

Tearing her eyes away from him, Harriet looked at
his companion whom she immediately recognised as the
woman in the photograph which she had used for the
leaflet—Jake's fiancée, Magda Thorne. There was no
doubt that Magda was a startlingly beautiful woman,
with short black curly hair surrounding a perfect oval
face, whose pale creamy skin had a luminescent glow.
The American model girl's slim frame was swathed in a
tight-fitting, white silk jersey dress that left little to the
imagination. She'd better be careful not to take a deep
breath, or she'll burst out and expose her all! Harriet
thought sourly, and then was ashamed of herself for
being so bitchy. Why should she care about Jake's

fiancée? And it was certainly none of her business what the woman was wearing, for heaven's sake!

Making an effort to stop looking at Magda who seemed so cool and sophisticated as she talked to a small, portly man, Harriet's eyes flicked sideways, widening in fright as she realised that while she had been so absorbed in gazing at his fiancée, Jake had been staring straight at her!

At that moment she nearly turned and bolted from the room. However, as she stood momentarily rooted to the floor, it became borne in upon her that Jake hadn't recognised her, or at least was having considerable difficulty in reconciling her present appearance with that of the girl he had met earlier in the day. He was frowning, his arctic blue eyes narrow with concentration as he ignored his companions, gazing fixedly at the tall girl across the room. Some moments later it seemed that he had made up his mind, turning to say something to the man beside him before beginning to move determinedly across the room towards Harriet.

Realising that it was too late for flight, she stood numbly waiting for disaster to strike. And then, when only a few yards away, she saw that his attention had been distracted by a flunkey, who indicated that he was expected to withdraw into a private ante-room reserved for the Master of the Livery Company and his personal guests. Jake hesitated for a moment, and then shrugged before returning to Magda's side and leading her away.

Harriet nearly sagged with relief, her legs still trembling as she accompanied her uncle into dinner. The magnificently decorated Egyptian room where the three hundred guests were seated for the meal blurred before Harriet's eyes. She was oblivious to the heavy crystal chandeliers and the string quartet up in the gallery, while the delicious food might have been ashes for all she knew or cared. Her whole being seemed

absorbed by Jake's dark head as he sat at the top table, far away across the room. She seemed somehow extraordinarily attuned to his every movement, and was immediately aware that while chatting politely to the guests on either side of him, his eyes were carefully and systematically searching each of the long tables. Sinking down in her seat, and praying that she would be shielded by her neighbour, she nevertheless knew that he had spotted her. It was as if his eyes had the ability to scorch and burn her skin even at that considerable distance, and when she eventually managed to look in his direction she found that she couldn't tear her gaze away from his.

At last the long evening seemed to be drawing to a close. The speeches were over, that of Jake being short, witty and amusing. The Master and his guests left the top table, and Harriet decided that it was definitely time for her to make good her escape. Hastily propelling her uncle down the stairs before her like one demented, she suddenly remembered that she had left her aunt's mink stole in the ladies' cloakroom. Commanding the bewildered, elderly man to go and wait for her in their chauffeured car, she sprinted around the corner.

Why on earth had she allowed her aunt to insist on her bringing that damn stole? Who needed to wear mink on a warm summer's evening, for heaven's sake? Almost screaming with frustration, she waited impatiently for the cloakroom lady to produce the garment before galloping through the large hall and out into the street. She had only taken two steps on to the pavement, before her arm was seized and she was swung around to face Jake's tall dark figure.

' "Well met by moonlight, fair Titania"—or in your case, Harriet, maybe "fair Cinderella" would be more appropriate, hmm . . .?' he murmured, his lips curving

into a sardonic smile as he viewed her shocked, pale face.

'That certainly was a sweet little interview you gave to that TV reporter, Harriet,' he continued grimly. 'I just caught it before leaving for this dinner tonight, and believe me, if I hadn't been the nasty villain of the piece, I'd have been crying my eyes out—alongside I don't know how many million other viewers! Thanks a bunch, sweetheart!'

Oh, God! Her uncle was waiting for her in the car, but he wouldn't sit there for ever. She had to get herself out of this—and fast! Drawing herself up to her full height of six feet, Harriet pretended to frown in puzzlement. 'I—I beg your pardon?' she drawled slowly. 'I don't believe we have been introduced.'

'Come off it, Harriet! I want to know what you're doing here,' he demanded curtly.

'My dear man. Kindly take your hand off my arm, or I shall be forced to call a member of the constabulary!'

Harriet's rich, plummy drawl—an accurate mimicry of her Aunt Clarissa at her most imperious—caused a flicker of doubt to cross Jake's face. A fact that she seized upon immediately.

'And my name is certainly not Harriet,' she continued, suddenly realising that she was, in some extraordinarily crazy and delirious fashion, actually enjoying the outrageous part she was playing. 'I will have you know, my good man, that I am Lady Ermintrude Bloodworthy, and if you do not let me go immediately, enabling me to join my husband who is waiting for me in our limousine, I shall have you arrested for molesting my person!'

' "*Lady Ermintrude Bloodworthy*" . . .?' Jake looked at her with stunned eyes, before throwing back his head and roaring with laughter. 'Oh Jesus, Harriet—you're priceless, you really are! In all my born days, I swear to

God I've never met such a crazy, totally bizarre girl! As for "molesting your person" . . .?' He was still laughing as he stepped back to gain a better view of her statuesque figure.

'You filthy cur! Get back to the gutter where you belong!' Harriet gestured imperiously, and then suddenly realising that he had let go of her arm, she picked up her skirts and sprinted hell for leather towards the car. Wrenching open the door she tumbled inside, breathlessly urging Simmons to drive home as fast as possible.

'My dear girl . . .' her uncle protested, his words cut short as Simmons did as he was told and both passengers were thrown back against the leather seats. Twisting around, Harriet looked out of the window to see Jake's tall figure clearly illuminated by a pool of light cast by a nearby street lamp. He was standing in the middle of the road, his hands on his hips, following the progress of the vintage Rolls Royce until it turned a corner and disappeared from sight.

Harriet sighed and leaned back in her chair. It had been a long, hard day in the law centre, and after that long session with Mrs O'Casey, she was feeling totally drained and exhausted. She was only supposed to have been offering general help for the morning session, but the lawyer in charge had been unexpectedly called away to a complicated court case, and the other girl with whom she worked had left to collect her children from school.

'I hate leaving you like this, Harry,' Sophie had said with a frown. 'Especially as we stay open until seven o'clock on a Friday night. Are you sure you'll be all right on your own? I can try and get back later if you like.'

'I'll be fine, and there's absolutely no need for you to

return,' Harriet had firmly assured her. She knew that Sophie, a qualified solicitor, was a single parent with two young children and was rushed off her feet, perpetually trying to be in two places at once.

Glancing down now at her watch, Harriet saw that it was half-past six. Only half an hour to go and then she could lock up and return to the flat and a long, hot bath. Deciding to make herself a strong cup of coffee, she rose from her desk and went through into the small, dank room at the back of the shop premises which had been lent to the law centre by a local worthy shopkeeper. Actually she reminded herself, he wasn't at all worthy! It was generally suspected that he was a receiver of stolen goods, but since the law centre was run on a shoe-string, with part-time solicitors giving their advice free to whoever needed it, they had agreed amongst themselves to turn a blind eye to the possibly criminal activities of their landlord.

Plugging in the electric kettle, Harriet leant wearily against the wall. It wasn't just today's traumatic session with Mrs O'Casey which was making her feel so tired and listless. For some reason, her life during the last two weeks had seemed almost unbearably dreary and difficult.

After the dinner in the Mansion House, Harriet had stayed the night in Eaton Square, arriving back at the house in King's Cross to find Andrew had just received the missing wheelchair—delivered by a chauffeur-driven Rolls Royce. It had been difficult, avoiding answering his question as to how Jake Lancaster knew where she lived; and it had soon become clear from Andrew's stiff, embarrassed attitude whenever they met, that their friendship wasn't going to return to normal. It was something that she very much regretted, but there was nothing she could do about it. Maybe, as time went by and Andrew found himself another girlfriend, they

would be able to return to their old, relaxed relationship. The fact that she wasn't seeing Andrew as often as in the past, and that she was working harder than ever in the law centre, had meant that when he did contact her about old Mrs Peters, the news had come as a considerable shock.

Why had she been such a cretinous fool? Why had she been so sure, so totally certain that Jake's word would be his bond? When he had said that he would clear up the matter of his subsidiary company's nefarious dealings, she had been quite confident that he meant what he said. In fact, so surprised had she been that she had rung his secretary, Miss Ann Norris.

Pretending to be the corrupt director's temporary typist, she had asked Miss Norris if she could check Mr Lancaster's appointments. 'I'm sure he was due to see our Mr Matthews this week,' Hariet said in a nasal, cockney accent. 'Only, you see, Mr Matthews has gorn and lost his diary, and I dunno who he's supposed to be seeing. Well, we don't want to upset Mr Lancaster by not knowing when he's coming to the office, do we dear?'

Miss Norris had been somewhat taken aback, but had quite freely supplied the information that far from making any appointment to see Mr Matthews, Mr Lancaster had flown off to Hong Kong and wouldn't be back until the sixteenth of June.

Slowly replacing the receiver, Harriet forced herself to acknowledge the fact that she had been conned. Maybe Jake had meant what he'd said at the time, but it was now clear that he wasn't going to do a damn thing about poor Mrs Peters and the other elderly residents in her road.

When the group of students who had demonstrated with her outside Lancaster International's offices met in her flat for a council of war, the air was blue with

rude expletives about Jake's behaviour. Quietly seated cross-legged on a floor cushion, Harriet felt far too apathetic to work up any righteous anger or indignation. She had already spent several sleepless nights trying to come to terms with her own shattered illusions, and quite unable to understand why she had fallen for his plausible assurances. The knowledge that she had been fooled was difficult to bear, but not nearly so painful as the slow realisation that she had *wanted* to believe Jake . . .

'Stop day-dreaming, Harry!' Rosie's voice had broken into her dismal thoughts. 'We've got this great idea for a mock funeral outside Mr Lancaster's offices. What do you think?'

'I don't think that's going to be any good,' she said slowly. 'Jake—I mean, Mr Lancaster—is away in Hong Kong at the moment, and if we do anything we ought to make sure it affects him personally. He's very much the boss and takes all the major decisions. Coming back from abroad to hear what has happened in his absence won't have nearly the same impact as if he'd experienced it personally . . .' her voice trailed away.

'Well, for goodness' sake think of something, Harry!' Andrew said with a return of his old spirit. 'I've never seen you so unenthusiastic before. Even Clarice over there seems to have more life in her than you do!'

Amidst the general laughter, Harriet looked over at Clarice. The white cockatoo was whistling quietly and rocking to and fro on her perch. Watching the bird, Harriet suddenly remembered Mrs Peters' two budgerigars of whom the old lady was so fond, and an idea began to form in her mind.

'Okay,' she said, 'I think I've got a plan. Although, after being so wrong about Mr Lancaster last time, there's no way I can guarantee that it will work,' she warned them.

'We can't just do nothing,' Rosie said. 'So, spill the beans and let's see if we think it's a goer.'

Having told them what she had in mind, and when they had all stopped laughing, there was total agreement that it would, at the very least, succeed in making Jake Lancaster's life extremely uncomfortable.

'It's a great wheeze, and I'm really sorry that we won't be able to be there to see his face!' Andrew chortled. 'The only problem is—how can we afford it? I reckon it's going to cost quite a lot of money, one way and another.'

'Look, why don't you leave it to me?' Harriet said quickly. 'I've—er—I've got a lot of contacts who owe me some favours, and I'm sure I can get hold of what we need very cheaply, okay?'

The following morning she had made another 'phone call to Miss Norris, this time pretending to be ringing on behalf of Magda Thorne, who was longing to see her dear fiancé, and exactly what time did Mr Lancaster's plane land at Heathrow airport on the sixteenth of June?

It was clear, from the expressionless voice and reluctant response of his secretary, that she was not overfond of Jake's fiancée. Miss Norris is probably in love with her boss—the poor fool! Harriet thought grimly as she noted down the information about Jake's arrival.

The next few days had been spent telephoning around London as she put the plan into effect. It was a good idea, and she knew she ought to be enthusiastic and excited about annoying Jake. But her heart wasn't in it, somehow. Once or twice she had even caught herself trying to think of a good reason to abandon the whole enterprise; a traitorous impulse which she ruthlessly crushed.

Her dismal thoughts were interrupted as she realised

the kettle must have been boiling away for ages. The little room was filled with a cloud of white steam, and she was groping blindly for a mug and the tin of coffee, when she heard the door bell of the shop tinkle.

Serve you right for day dreaming, she told herself, abandoning her attempt to make herself a cup of coffee, and going back into the main office.

'I'm sorry to keep you waiting ... *What on earth are you doing here?*' she gasped, her eyes widening with shock at the sight of Jake's tall figure standing inside the door.

'Do you greet all your—er—clients with such enthusiasm?' he mocked, grinning at her as he walked over to put his briefcase down on her desk.

'Yes ... no ... I mean ...' She quickly gripped the back of her chair for support and took a deep breath. 'I was just surprised to—to see you here, that's all. What do you want?'

'How about some free legal advice?' he murmured with a lazy smile.

'Free advice ...? You must be off your rocker! People as rich as you can pay for whatever they need. And what are you doing here, anyway?' she demanded breathlessly. Her heart was pounding in her chest like a sledgehammer, and her knees were knocking like a pair of castanets as she saw Jake reach inside his jacket and remove a leather bound cheque book and fountain pen.

'Okay, how much?'

'How—how much ...?'

'You're a little slow on the uptake today, aren't you, Harriet?' He sat down at the desk. 'However, you are quite right, of course. A "bloated capitalist" such as myself, should indeed pay for legal advice. So how much do you want?'

She must be dreaming—it was a nightmare, that's what it was! Harriet told herself wildly as she stared

down into Jake's smiling face. For the first time she
noticed that he looked very tired. There seemed to be
shadows beneath his deep blue eyes and his skin was
pale beneath his tan. What on earth was he *really* doing
here? Had he come from his apartment, breathing hell-
fire and damnation because of what he'd found there?
No, of course he hadn't, or he wouldn't be smiling like
that. Oh God! What on earth was she to do? She must—
she simply must get rid of him as quickly as possible.

'I—I'm afraid that I can't help you. I can't possibly
take any money, it would be . . . um . . . yes, it would be
quite unprofessional of me to do so. I'm not fully
qualified yet, you see.'

'I quite understand.' Jake smiled and put his cheque
book and pen away. 'But you would be prepared to
give me some friendly advice if I needed it at any time,
wouldn't you?'

'Yes, yes, of course,' she muttered hurriedly. 'But
now, I'm afraid that you really must leave. I have to
close up this place and go home.'

'Do you have to go straight home? I was hoping you
would allow me to take you out to dinner.'

'*What?*'

'My dear girl, you've just promised me that you'd
give me some friendly advice . . .'

'I certainly did not!' she snapped.

'Oh, yes, you definitely did. And it would be far more
pleasant to discuss matters over a meal than in these
surroundings, don't you think?'

'But I can't!' She wailed. 'I have to go back and feed
my animals, and . . . and . . .'

'There's no problem. I will drive you home. Come on,
hurry up and get a move on. If those animals of yours
are as hungry and tired as I am, we have no time to
lose!'

Jake was like a steamroller, firmly overriding all her

frantic objections, so that five minutes later she found herself seated in his long low sports car. Laying her weary head against the back-rest, Harriet closed her eyes and tried to convince herself that it really didn't matter if he took her back to the house, although she could only fervently pray that Andrew and the others would be out for the evening. How could she possibly explain why she was being driven around in Jake's car, when she didn't even know why, herself?

CHAPTER FOUR

'WELL, this apartment is certainly quite different to what I imagined.' Jake's voice floated through the open door of the small kitchen.

Nervously aware of his tall figure prowling around the living room, staring at the pictures on the walls and the long shelves of books, Harriet couldn't think clearly. She still wasn't sure how Jake had managed to persuade her to let him accompany her into the house, and when he had taken the keys from her hand and opened the door to her ground floor flat—well, it had somehow seemed pointless to continue objecting, especially since he didn't seem to be taking notice of anything she said.

On their arrival, Montmorency had rushed in from the garden like a rocket out of control, but even the dog's loud barking and the way he had leaped up leaving dusty footprints all over Jake's smart dark suit, hadn't appeared to disturb the damn man's composure. 'Down, boy!' Jake had said firmly, and what had the traitorous animal done, but promptly—and for the first time in his life—obeyed a command!

It was only too obvious that Montmorency was a rotten judge of character, Harriet told herself gloomily, jabbing a tin opener into the can of dog meat. If ever an animal didn't deserve his supper—'Ouch!' she muttered, looking down to see that she had cut her finger on a jagged piece of metal.

It had been a ghastly day, and it looked like getting worse, she thought grimly, hunting through a kitchen drawer for a plaster to put on her finger. How on earth

was she to get rid of Jake? Luckily, it seemed as though Andrew and the rest of the students were out for the evening, but if they should return while he was still here, they'd never understand that the impossible man had practically highjacked her again. She wasn't entirely sure how her friends would react, but they were bound to take a very dim view of her consorting with someone whom they regarded as 'the enemy'.

But that was only part of the problem. She had allowed plenty of time for a possible flight delay, and for Jake's journey from Heathrow to his penthouse suite overlooking Hyde Park, but it looked as if he must have caught an earlier plane. However, she was certain that he hadn't been home yet, and if she managed to get rid of him within the next hour, the carefully laid plans she had instigated might still have had a chance of working.

Resolutely hardening her heart against an instinctive feeling that she was somehow behaving like a Judas, she called Montmorency to come and have his supper, and walked slowly towards the living room, pausing on the threshold as Jake turned to look at her.

He had removed the jacket of his dark suit, revealing a white silk shirt that clung to his broad, powerful shoulders like a second skin. He was looking impossibly handsome, and she suddenly thought that he must either exercise regularly or be naturally slim, because there wasn't an ounce of fat on his lean, muscular body.

Harriet swallowed hard and tried to pull herself together, walking into the room with an air of assumed nonchalance. 'Would you like a drink?' she asked.

'Yes, indeed I would. You seem to have an interesting collection of music,' he added, bending to pick up a record sleeve from the rack by her stereo. 'If, after our first meeting, I'd been asked what sort of classical music would appeal to you—well, I guess I'd

have picked something dramatic like Beethoven or
Wagner, for instance. I certainly wouldn't have expected
to find Bach, Telemann or Vivaldi.'

'Is that supposed to be significant?' she muttered,
struggling to control her rapid heartbeat and the
quickening of her pulse.

'It's very unemotional music—meticulously tidy, if
you like. Rather like this apartment,' he smiled, and
looking around at the colourful, neatly arranged sofas,
tables and chairs. 'And "unemotional", my dear
Harriet, is not how I see you at all!'

Harriet gave a dismissive shrug. 'Your remark seems
to call for that well-known cliché: appearances can be
deceptive.'

'Hmm ... well, I certainly can't fault your
appearance today!' He smiled as his eyes flicked over
her slim, cornflower blue shirtwaister dress. 'You look
good enough to eat,' he murmured, and before she
could think of a suitable reply, he turned away to
regard with interest the large white bird standing
immobile on a perch, its head tucked under a wing.
'This looks like a cockatoo. Is it stuffed?'

'Certainly not—and don't you upset Clarice by
saying so! She's just shy, that's all,' Harriet explained,
going over to tickle the back of the bird's neck.

'And what's that?' he asked, pointing to a cage filled
with sawdust and shredded paper. As he spoke, a very
small rat-like animal emerged from a wooden shelter
within the box, and climbed into a small wheel which it
proceeded to revolve very quickly.

' "That" is a gerbil,' Harriet said over her shoulder as
she walked away across the room. 'I'm afraid that I
don't have much in the way of alcohol, just some
whisky and white wine.'

'A neat scotch will be fine,' Jake murmured,
continuing to stare with fascination at the small gerbil

whizzing around inside the wheel. 'Okay, I've met Montmorency and—er—Clarice, I think you said her name was. So what's this cute little fellow called?'

'I was only asked to look after him a few days ago, when one of the students in the house went abroad, so I haven't really thought of a name yet,' she explained tersely, coming over to hand him a whisky.

'Well, I am surprised to hear that.' He gave her a wide, sardonic grin. 'I would have thought that a girl, who can pluck a name like "Lady Ermintrude Bloodworthy" out of the air at a moment's notice, would have no difficulty in naming this tiny creature!'

Harriet gasped, her hands shaking so much that she nearly dropped her wine glass. 'I—I don't know what you're talking about,' she muttered, turning away to pick up a book which had fallen on the floor. How could she have forgotten that crazy meeting outside the Mansion House? She might be feeling very tired, but there was no excuse for not realising that he was bound to bring up the matter. She must be going soft in the head!

'Actually,' she drawled breathlessly, making a valiant effort to change the subject, and cursing the fact that she wasn't managing to sound as sophisticated as she would have liked. 'You haven't met everyone who lives here. There's Fred, the parrot. He's hiding at the moment because he's very choosy who he meets—and he particularly dislikes strange men who barge their way into this flat.'

'Like his mistress?'

'Exactly!'

Jake gave a low laugh. 'My dear Harriet, we may have only had two—er—extraordinary meetings, but I assure you that I can recall every riveting moment of our brief, if somewhat bizarre, acquaintanceship! So you can hardly call me a stranger. Besides which, how

could I possibly not remember meeting such a beautiful girl, hmm?'

Her head jerked up at the warm, sensuous note in his voice, alarm bells ringing in her brain as they chimed out the message: *This man is dangerous!*

'Good gracious, Mr Lancaster! You're very free with your compliments today. Do correct me if I'm wrong, but I was under the impression that you thought of me as a scumbag.'

'Ouch! I guess I deserved that.'

Jake was shaking his head sorrowfully, but there was nothing wrong with her eye-sight, and she was perfectly well aware of the laughter dancing in his blue eyes—damn him!

'Yes, you did,' she said grimly. 'And when you've finished your drink, I would be pleased if you'd leave.' She paused as an inspired thought flashed through her brain, and it was all she could do to try and keep her face straight. 'However, before you go, I feel I really must reciprocate by paying *you* a compliment.'

'Really?' He frowned, his eyes narrowing warily as she threw him a brilliant smile.

'Really and truly. I'm sure you'll be pleased to know that I've decided to name the gerbil after you. "Jake" will be a perfect name for him, because he's just like a certain high-powered businessman I know—always so busy trundling away on his little wheel, that he hasn't a clue what's going on beyond his cage. And when he's not doing that, he spends the rest of his life shredding paper!'

Harriet almost ground her teeth with frustration when she saw that far from succeeding in annoying him, Jake was finding the idea uproariously funny. 'You are, without doubt, the most unusual and amusing girl I've ever met!'

'I have no idea how many girls you've met. But I

would be surprised if you have ever met anyone who is quite so angry with you as I am!'

The laughter died from his face as he registered the suppressed fury in her voice. 'For heaven's sake— what's wrong?'

'What's wrong, is that I was stupid enough to believe you when you said that you'd sort out that rotten company of yours, Metropolitan Development. Mr Jason Lancaster's word is certainly not his bond, is it?' Harriet made no effort to hide her icy contempt. 'You've done absolutely nothing about the matter—but then, why should you care? No one is going to pull down your nice, luxurious home, are they?'

'Oh, God!' Jake hit his forehead with the flat of his palm. 'I completely forgot.'

Harriet gave a short, contemptuous laugh. 'Who are you kidding? You never had any intention of doing a damn thing about it.'

'That's not true!' he protested, putting down his drink and coming over to stand looking down at her. 'Believe me, I have every intention of sorting the matter out, but . . .'

'Rubbish! However, if it's any consolation, you'll be glad to hear that while I may be angry with you, it's nothing compared to how furious I am with myself for thinking you meant what you said. How could I have been such an idiot?'

'Look, why don't you shut that sweet mouth of yours for a moment, and just listen to me,' he snapped, putting his hands firmly on her shoulders. 'I was not lying when I said that I'm going to sort this matter out.'

'Hah!' At her snort of derision, his fingers tightened on her slim shoulders like fierce talons.

'You God-damned, stupid girl!' Jake grated angrily. 'There was no time to go into the matter on the day you came to see me—the day of the Annual General

Meeting, okay? And that night I had to attend a dinner and give a speech in the Mansion House, an occasion we can both vividly remember; although why and for what reason you persist in claiming amnesia about that episode, is quite beyond me at the moment. However, when I got home, I found an urgent telex message awaiting me, which meant I had to fly to Hong Kong at six o'clock the next morning. And for your information: the moment I landed back here in England, late this afternoon, I came straight from the airport to see you.'

He paused, tense and tight-lipped, his cheeks flushed as he stared down at her with blue eyes that glinted coldly like sharp points of ice. 'You're a smart girl, Harriet. So, maybe you can tell me *exactly* when I had the time to sort out such a delicate business. Or do you think I should have telephoned Mr Matthews from Hong Kong and had a long, friendly discussion about graft and corruption, with probably half the world listening in?'

Unable to meet his penetrating, intense gaze, Harriet closed her eyes as her head drooped wearily. Jake's fierce verbal assault had totally shattered her frail defences against his dominant personality. Not only were her nerves at screaming point, but she felt almost sick with mental exhaustion and confusion. With a timetable like that, he obviously hadn't had time to see to Mrs Peters—or was he lying again? Of course not—why should he bother? Maybe, because he didn't want a scandal in the newspapers, and so keeping her quiet would be a good idea . . .? The pros and cons of the case surged back and forth in her tired brain, but always she came back to the same point. She wanted— oh, how she wanted to believe him.

'Well?' Jake shook her roughly.

'I—I just don't know what to think anymore,' she cried, twisting away from beneath his cruel fingers, and

stumbling over to lean against the sliding door to the courtyard, resting her heated forehead on the cool plate glass window.

'Please try and be reasonable,' Jake said quietly behind her. 'I'd be a fool to ignore your very serious accusations against a director of one of my companies. But here in England, as in America, surely a person is innocent until he's proved guilty, right? I can't just charge in like the Keystone Kops. I have to investigate the matter, and then deal with whatever it is that I find. As for your Mrs Peters, I'm quite sure that they haven't pulled her house down while I've been away.'

'But you still don't understand . . .' Harriet wailed huskily, her face hidden from his view by her heavy chestnut hair. 'It's just a collection of bricks and mortar to someone like you, but for an old lady like Elsie Peters, it—it's the centre of her universe. Can't you see that it's her *home* . . .?'

There didn't seem to be anything Harriet could do to prevent the tears from streaming down her face, her body shaken by deep sobs that racked her slim frame.

She was dimly aware of Jake muttering a violent oath under his breath, and then she felt his arms closing about her shaking, trembling figure. 'I'm s-so s-sorry . . .' she muttered helplessly, leaning her head weakly against his broad shoulder.

'Hush, sweetheart. There's no need to cry,' he murmured softly, lifting a hand to gently brush a tendril of hair from her brow. 'Come and sit down,' he added, leading her towards a large sofa covered in faded red velvet. Continuing to hold her in his firm embrace, Jake quietly waited until the storm of tears diminished.

'I'm so ashamed . . .' she muttered. 'I c-can't think why . . .'

'Now, that's enough,' he said gently but firmly, taking out a large handkerchief to wipe the droplets of

tears from her damp eyelashes. 'So, be a good girl and blow your nose, hmm?' he added, handing her the large square of white cotton.

'Yes, thank you,' she sniffed, giving him a wobbly, watery smile as she did as she was told. Her body was still shaken by occasional hiccups as she closed her eyes, and like a tired child snuggled up against the warmth of his hard chest, firmly held within the total security of the arms clasped about her slim figure. How long she lay there, savouring the comfort of his warm skin through the fine silk shirt, the feel of his hand as he gently stroked her hair, she had no idea.

'I think you'd better tell me what's wrong, Harriet,' he murmured at last, settling her more comfortably in his arms so that he could see her face. 'I reckon that you're normally a fairly sensible, rational sort of girl—even if you are a bit crazy sometimes!—and so I guess that there's more to these tears than just old Mrs Peters, sad though her case is.'

'Did you really come straight from the airport to see me?' she asked dreamily, the storm of weeping having left her feeling extraordinarily light-headed.

Jake gave a low rumble of laughter. 'I can see that your feminine instincts are in good shape, sweetheart! However, let's take one thing at a time. I want you to tell me why you're so upset.'

That's the second time he's called me 'sweetheart', but maybe it doesn't mean anything in America . . .? Harriet mused drowsily, before she felt Jake give her a slight, impatient shake and she forced herself to sit up straight.

'Yes,' she sighed heavily, staring down at her pale hands clasped so firmly by his strong, brown fingers. 'I suppose it was Mrs O'Casey, really. I—I've been desperately trying to shut it out of my mind, you see,' she raised her large grey eyes to his.

'No, I don't see,' he said with a warm, patient smile. 'So, tell me all about it, hmm?'

'I suppose being a lawyer is something like being a doctor. We've had it dinned into us, times without number, that we mustn't become too involved in the problems of the people we are trying to help. It—well, it has to be good advice, but it's sometimes easier said than done.' She grabbed the handkerchief and blew her nose.

'Well, poor Mrs O'Casey came to see me this afternoon, with her three children, and—and it was so awful, you've no idea! She was so thin and hopeless, and I've never seen such skinny, pale children, or any who looked so nervous and frightened. She's a battered wife, you see—actually, they were all battered. It—it nearly broke my heart to see how the children jumped and looked scared everytime a heavy lorry went by, or a car backfired in the street. And there was absolutely n-nothing I could d-do to help them . . .'

Once again she couldn't seem to stop the tears from welling up in her eyes. 'I tried. I really did everything I could to persuade her to take the children and go to stay in sheltered housing. But she was too frightened to leave her husband. "He'd find us and kill us if we went there", she kept on saying. You see, she'd come to the law centre in the hope that Mr O'Casey could be put safely away in prison, and when she found out that he couldn't—well, not immediately, anyway—she just gave up hope. Oh Jake—I felt so impotent! Those poor little children . . .!'

'My sweet Harriet, you've got a heart like a hotel,' he murmured, once more wiping her tears away. 'Now, I want you to listen to me,' he added firmly. 'First of all, how old are you?'

'Almost t-twenty-two.'

'Well, it may seem a great age to you, but not when

looked at in the context of what was clearly needed here—a mature, knowledgeable lawyer. Yes, of course meeting such an unhappy and unfortunate lady was deeply distressing. How could it be otherwise? But qualified lawyers, with some years of practice under their belt, are used to seeing people in that state. You've had no experience of this sort of thing, and you are still far too young and tender hearted to deal with it. Maybe you will be able to cope with such a disturbing case in time, but not now. Can't you see that you've been trying to run before you've even learned to walk? And whoever allowed a kid like you to work in that law centre should be shot!' he added grimly.

'I just wanted to do something to help people who aren't as well off as I am. But I don't seem to be very good at it, do I?' she sighed heavily.

'For God's sake, Harriet—haven't you been listening to a word I've said?' Jake said roughly, putting his hands on either side of her head, and turning her face towards his. 'You're a sweet, warm, loving girl. And in the fullness of time you'll be able to cope with the Mrs O'Casey's of this world. But not just now, not yet. Understand?'

She nodded, realising that what he said was right and sensible. But she couldn't seem to hang on to her concentration, not when his thumbs were gently caressing the soft skin beneath her cheek bones, and his blue eyes were gleaming in the same way as they had in the underground car park, two weeks ago.

The room was suddenly so still and silent, that she was vividly aware of every tiny sound: the evening traffic outside in the street, the tick-tock of the clock on the mantelpiece, the small scratching noise across the room as Clarice picked at her birdseed. Harriet's lips parted, breathless and trembling with a sensual awareness which ached within her. Gazing at his face,

which seemed suddenly pale beneath the tan, her eyes were drawn like a magnet to the warm hard curve of his mouth. And then she was lost, shuddering with a burning need that transcended all thought as Jake drew her softly towards him, lowering his dark head to brush his mouth across her quivering lips.

'Jake, I . . .' was all she managed to say before his lips closed over hers, his hands moving through the heavy mass of her wavy chestnut hair to hold her head firmly beneath him. His mouth was cool, moving gently over hers at first as though he was carefully controlling himself; but as she trembled helplessly in his arms, swept by a rising tide of desire that shattered what remained of her senses, she provoked a low groan deep in his throat and his kiss deepened. Shuddering with excitement beneath the rampant sensuality of his lips, her arms crept up to wind themselves about his head, burying her fingers in the thick dark hair as she responded ardently and passionately to the invasive mastery of his tongue.

She gave a small moan of disappointment when he lifted his head, gently cupping her face in his strong hands as he stared intently down into her dazed eyes. 'God knows how much I've been wanting to do that for the past two weeks,' he murmured hoarsely, his long brown fingers moving slowly and softly over the fine contours of her face, as if he were blind and he needed to imprint the memory of her features into his brain.

'But you can't . . . I mean, you're getting married,' she whispered, closing her eyes and almost choking from a hard lump which seemed to be obstructing her throat.

She heard him sigh, 'That's my problem, not yours,' as he gently touched the corner of her mouth with his lips before trailing them down the long column of her

neck, seeking the scented hollows at the base of her throat.

'No . . .!' she gasped, shaken by a sudden spasm of fright as she felt his hands caressing the soft, full swell of her breasts, unconfined beneath her thin cotton dress; the fear quickly giving way to a heated wave of erotic excitement which surged through her veins at his intimate touch.

'Sweet Harriet!' he muttered thickly in her ear, his breath ragged, quickening in response to the yielding warmth of her body. 'The thought of you has been driving me wild! How I want to—*My God! What's that . . .?*'

Jake's sudden, loud exclamation of horror coincided with a swish of beating wings as a large grey object landed on the sofa beside his head. Looking up, his vision was filled with the sight of angry dark eyes and a sharp, curved beak as a bird began sidling menacingly towards him.

'Who's a silly billy . . .? I'll have your guts for garters . . .!' the bird croaked malevolently, and Jake, with what he could only think of afterwards as demonstrating remarkable presence of mind, leaped to his feet and backed swiftly away.

Drowning with ecstasy one moment, Harriet was jerked forcibly out of her mindless state the next, hearing Jake's violent reaction to Fred, the parrot, at the same time as she found herself thrown roughly back against the sofa cushions. Blushing a deep crimson, she struggled to sit up, clutching the top of her dress which seemed to have come apart, and feverishly attempting to do up the buttons with fingers that trembled as though she had palsy.

'For God's sake!' Jake thundered. 'This is no time for maidenly modesty—just call off that creature!' He gestured wildly towards the parrot who was now

making a loud, whistling noise that sounded exactly like an aeroplane diving out of the skies.

'It's all right, it's only Fred,' she murmured. And then, as she looked at the parrot rocking himself violently to and fro, and at Jake's expression of outrage and indignation, she was unable to stop herself from giggling.

'I'm glad you find it so funny!' he snarled. 'My God—that parrot sounds just like a divebomber. I tell you, it's nothing more or less than World War Two in this damned apartment! One crazy girl, and God knows how many weirdly exotic and downright dangerous animals. I . . .' Words seemed to fail him as he pushed his hands roughly through his hair.

'I—I'm sorry . . .' Harriet gasped helplessly, her body racked by gales of laughter. 'I know it's not f-funny, b-but . . .' and then she couldn't say any more, clutching her stomach and aching with the effort to contain her mirth.

'Yes, well, I suppose I do look a bit ridiculous, being scared by a bird!' Jake's lips twitched as his shock gradually subsided, although he still kept a wary eye on the aggressive bird now perched on a high bookshelf, and muttering quietly under its breath.

'Maybe it's just as well, hmm?' he added, coming over to sit down beside Harriet, who was lying back against the cushions and feeling totally exhausted.

'It was a rotten thing to do, to laugh at you like that,' she said quietly. 'But I honestly couldn't help it.' She hesitated, evading his piercing eyes which were fixed intently on her face. If only she'd had more experience of this sort of situation, she might be able to throw off a careless, witty comment or a light remark that positively dripped with sophistication. As it was, she felt hideously awkward and embarrassingly aware of a deep flush staining her cheeks. Quickly rising to her

feet, she walked over to stare out into the small garden which was cloaked by long, dark evening shadows. 'I think you'd better go now, don't you?' she muttered without turning around.

Jake didn't answer immediately as he came to stand silently behind her, lifting a lock of her brilliant hair and giving a heavy sigh as he ran it softly through his fingers. 'Yes,' he murmured quietly, slowly turning her to face him before bending forward to plant a gentle kiss on her forehead.

Watching him walk across the room to put on his jacket, Harriet couldn't remember when she had last felt so miserable. Was Jake now going straight from her to his fiancée? Was Magda Thorne waiting impatiently for him, back in his apartment ...? As the question flitted through her tired, unhappy mind, Harriet gasped with dismay. She had completely forgotten all about the plans she had made and put into effect! She couldn't possibly let him leave, not without warning him—even if Andrew and his friends never talked to her again.

'Um ... er ... Jake, I think that I ought to—to tell you that ... um ... I'm afraid you aren't going to be very pleased when you get home. In fact,' she added with a rush, 'I think you will be very angry indeed. I'm very sorry, but I—that is, we—thought you had forgotten all about Mrs Peters, and ...' she gestured helplessly.

Jake turned and gave her a hard, searching look. 'Okay—what have you done now? Burned the apartment building down?'

'No, of course not. Arson's a felony, carrying a long prison sentence,' she muttered, staring down at the floor.

'*Oh, great!* We mustn't break the law, is that it?' He gave a harsh, cruel laugh. 'Okay, Harriet, I guess I'll find out soon enough exactly what particular idea of

genius you've come up with this time. So just leave me in suspense until I get home, will you? Otherwise, it's very likely that I'll be found guilty—here and now—of infanticide!'

'Jake!' she gasped, but he didn't hear her strangled cry as he stormed out of the flat, slamming the door loudly behind him.

Jake's grip tightened on the driving wheel, his knuckles white with tension as he cursed the slow-moving traffic. God knows what he was going to find when he got home. That crazy, quite abominable girl, Harriet, was capable of anything—*absolutely anything!* Ever since the day of his company's annual meeting, when Harriet had organised and mounted that impudent, not to say quite preposterous demonstration outside his offices, his well-ordered, civilised existence seemed to have been turned upside-down.

Quickly slamming his foot down hard on the brake as a small foreign car cut in sharply in front of him, Jake swore out loud before taking a deep breath and telling himself that he must try and calm down. There was no point in driving recklessly and killing either himself or another person, just because he was in a blind rage with that irresponsible, eccentric girl. She was quite clearly a mental case who should have been locked up years ago!

Some ten minutes later, Jake sighed and leaned back in his seat as he waited for some traffic lights to change. The soft strains of Beethoven's *Pastoral* symphony, issuing from the car stereo, were having a relaxing, soothing effect on his anger as he realised that it was pointless to continue fulminating about what he was likely to find when he returned to his apartment. Knowing Harriet, it could be anything—from another student demonstration to a dancing bear! The hard, angular planes of his face softened momentarily, his lips

twisting with grim amusement as he recalled the extraordinarily weird sight she had presented, when they had first met outside his offices.

What on earth had come over him lately? Okay, maybe he had been experiencing a certain dissatisfaction with his lifestyle; had been occasionally asking himself whether taking on more and more companies, and expanding his financial empire was destined to be the sum total of his existence. Not that it would have occurred to him to question the even tenor of his life if, when he had last paid a visit to his mother back in America, she hadn't roundly condemned him for being nothing more or less than a workaholic.

'There are worse things to be,' he had replied, smiling fondly at the small white-haired, imperious woman.

'Not if you are in danger of becoming a bore, Jake!' she had swiftly retorted. 'And, in a few years time, that's exactly what you will be,' she added as he raised a dark eyebrow and looked at her with incredulity.

'Oh, come on . . .'

'When do you ever think of anything but business?' she continued inexorably. 'Oh, yes, I know that you're seen in all the right places with a beautiful girl on your arm, but you don't seem to take any of them very seriously, do you? Certainly not enough to settle down and marry one of them, and give me some grand-children.'

Jake laughed. 'You're impossible, Mother! You've already got two granddaughters . . .'

'Whom I hardly see, since your sister lives on the other side of the country,' his mother retorted sharply. 'Besides, you are being deliberately obtuse. You know very well that I was referring to *your* children—sons who will carry on the family name and the family business.'

'I might well produce nothing but daughters. Have you thought of that?' he teased.

His mother waved dismissively. 'I'm not going to let you sidetrack me, Jake. You're a wealthy, sophisticated man, whom I'm proud to call my son, but are you really happy with your calm, civilised and oh-so-predictably boring way of life?'

'Yes, of course I am,' he said quickly. 'Ever since Father died and there was that epic struggle for control of the company—which was not an entirely *boring* situation!—I've been far too busy to think of such things as getting married. However, if you're set on having more grandchildren, I suppose I'd better do something about it.'

'Oh, for heaven's sakes!' his mother gave him an exasperated smile. 'There you go again: "and the next item on my agenda" . . .! Yes, of course I hope to live long enough to bounce your children on my knees, but that's not the main reason why I want you to fall in love and get married. Can't you see that, despite all your wealth, the apartments in Manhattan and London, not to mention the estates both here, in Connecticut, and that large place you've bought in England—none of that matters a damn unless you've got the right person to share it with.' She looked at his bland, smiling expression and sighed heavily. 'What you need, my dear boy, is someone who will occasionally ruffle and disturb those cool feathers of yours.'

'God forbid!' he had laughed, before adroitly changing the subject on to other matters about which they could agree. However, he had taken heed of his mother's advice, and she had subsequently seemed very happy and content with his engagement to the beautiful international model, Magda Thorne.

'Ruffle my feathers, indeed!' He gave a harsh laugh as the traffic lights changed and he drew away from the

kerb. His mother couldn't have been more hideously wrong. For instance, he needed someone like Harriet in hs life, like a hole in the head! She'd burst into his calm existence like a firework out of control, and had proceeded to cause the maximum possible disruption in a very short space of time. The deeply disturbing fact that he felt an overwhelming, sexual attraction to the extraordinary girl, was just an unfortunate example of the way such a maverick emotion could affect even the very best, most reasonable of men.

So, he'd deal in a cool, calm manner with whatever trouble Harriet had cooked up for him this time, and that would be it, he promised himself grimly. Definitely and absolutely *it*!

Driving into the underground car park of the large modern apartment building, he tossed the car keys to the attendant and walked through into the foyer. The lift seemed to take an age to reach his penthouse apartment, although as he stood outside his front door he breathed a sigh of relief to find that everything looked fairly normal. Maybe Harriet had been teasing him after all, he thought as he put the key in the lock.

'Oh there you are, sir. I was wondering . . .'

Jake was able to barely glance at his manservant's worried face, before he cursed aloud at the sharp pain as his knee met a hard metal obstruction.

'For God's sake, Carter—what's this thing doing in the hall?' he demanded, staring down at the unfamiliar object.

'Oh that, sir. Yes, well, I'm very sorry to have left it there. It has only just been delivered you see, although I have managed to place the other seven similar items in the dining room.'

'But what is it?'

'Ahem.' Carter gave a delicate cough. 'I rather think

that they are a form of mobile calor gas heater, sir. I must express some surprise that you should have felt the need to buy such things. They are not at all what I am used to. But then, I can't say that I have ever looked after a gentleman who wished to decorate his drawing room with twelve cages of budgerigars, either.'

'*Budgerigars . . .?*' Jake looked at him in astonishment. 'What on earth are they?'

'Singing birds, sir.' Carter's voice was heavy with disapproval. 'I understand that they are very popular among the lower echelons of society. Of course, Siamese cats are perfectly acceptable—in their way. But ten of them, Mr Lancaster, is really going too far!' he added with a sniff before leading the way into the large drawing-room.

'Good God!' Jake exclaimed, looking around him with dazed eyes.

'Exactly, sir! Now, if you had expressed a wish to possess a bird of some kind, I would not have felt it beneath me to have arranged for a nice quiet canary to be delivered, for instance. Although I would not have advised having a resident cat at the same time. They can be very vicious, Siamese cats can, and let loose among all those birds—well, sir, I really don't fancy the consequences. It would be nothing more or less than a carnage!' He shuddered. 'I have consequently left them in their wicker baskets for the time being. But really, Mr Lancaster, *it will not do!*'

'You are absolutely right, Carter. I don't know where they came from, but they must be got rid of immediately,' Jake agreed swiftly, wishing that Harriet was present so that he could personally wring her neck. It was obvious that if he didn't sort this business out very quickly, he risked losing the services of his manservant. Carter was invaluable and they both knew that Jake would be lost without him.

'May I also send back the heaters and the cases of stout, sir?'

'Stout? What in the hell is that? Oh God—the noise in here! If those damn birds don't stop chirping . . . and what's making those dreadful crying sounds?' he added, putting his hands over his ears for a moment.

'The Siamese cats. I understand that they make that noise when they are disturbed or unhappy, Mr Lancaster. As for the dozen cases of stout—I took the liberty of putting them away in the larder. Stout is a very heavy dark ale, and I once worked for a gentleman who liked to drink it with champagne, so it occurred to me that you might have decided to do the same.'

'No way, Carter. I'll take my champagne neat, thank you. But you can give me a very strong scotch on the rocks right away—and why don't you have one yourself?'

As his manservant left the room, Jake looked about him. Nothing could possibly look more peculiar or outlandish than the sight of twelve cages on their chrome metal stands dotted about the carefully designed, ultra-modern furnishings of his apartment. The decor had been featured in some of the most prestigious magazines on home decoration, and the lacquer tables had obviously not been designed to display ten wicker baskets full of screaming cats. He turned as Carter returned, seizing up the glass and downing its contents without pausing for breath.

'Keep them coming, I've a feeling I'm going to need all the alcohol I can get hold of tonight!' Jake said grimly.

'I don't blame you, sir,' the older man said sympathetically, wincing at the noise in the room. 'Oh, yes, these cards came with the goods when they were delivered.'

Jake slit the envelopes open, but he didn't need to

read the cards they contained to know *exactly* who had sent them. Killing is too good for that girl—I'll boil her alive if I get the chance, he told himself as he read the messages. They were all substantially the same. The one sent with the birds read: 'When Mrs Elsie Peters is thrown out into the street, she won't have a home for her budgerigar'. The others were similar, pointing out that Mrs Peters wouldn't be able to drink her stout in comfort, neither could she afford to pay for her heating, or have a home for her cat.

He was still trying to think how he was going to get rid of the birds and cats, when Carter entered the room. 'There's a man here who insists on seeing you. He says it is urgent, sir.'

'Oh, God, all right. I'd better see him in the study, or I won't be able to hear a word he's saying.'

Carter looked uneasy. 'Ahem. I fear that I omitted to mention the twenty large potted plants, Mr Lancaster.'

'Don't tell me . . .'

'Yes, sir, I'm afraid so. They're in the study.'

'*Great!* That's all I need. Is there any room that isn't filled with something diabolical?' Jake raged as the telephone rang beside where he was standing.

'Yes, who is it?' he snapped. 'Oh, I'm sorry, Magda . . . yes, I know I was supposed to ring you . . . look, I really can't talk now . . . no, of course I haven't got another woman here—I only wish I had! No . . . no I didn't mean it that way . . . no, I can't make it tonight . . . yes, you are absolutely right, I've had a few drinks and I fully intend to have a good many more . . . if you must know, I'm trying to deal with twelve budgerigars, ten Siamese cats, God knows how many potted plants—not to mention some mobile heaters and cases of stout! . . . Well, if you don't believe me, that's just too damn bad!' he shouted, slamming down the 'phone.

'*Women!*' he ground out through clenched teeth before stalking out of the room.

Returning to the living room, having with some considerable difficulty persuaded the man from a removal company that he had no intention of moving to a house off the Old Caledonian Road—wherever that might be—he accepted another drink from Carter.

'If I could just get my hand on her throat, I'd throttle the wretched girl to death!' he growled, sipping his drink while his manservant busied himself placing various kitchen cloths over the birdcages.

'Miss Thorne?' Carter murmured, not looking unduly upset by the fate which appeared to face his employer's wife-to-be.

'No, of course not. I was thinking of a certain Miss Harriet Drummond.'

'Of Drummond and Harleys Bank? Now, there's a nice young girl for you, sir. Very wealthy, I understand. You could do a lot worse.'

'For God's sake, Carter! For positively the last time, will you stop trying to marry me off to what you call "nice girls!" Kindly get it into your head, and accept the fact that I'm engaged to Miss Thorne. Okay?' Jake brushed his hands wearily through his hair. 'Besides, this is definitely one time you've got your wires crossed. You may think you know *Who's Who* backwards, but the Harriet Drummond I've had the misfortune to meet is not at all "nice", lives in a street you wouldn't be seen dead in, and needs a good thrashing once a week and twice on Sundays!'

Carter didn't deign to reply, his employer being obviously tired from his flight, and all that had happened since his return to the apartment. Leaving the room in dignified silence, he returned minutes later with a small parcel which had just been delivered by special messenger.

'What else can it be, but a bomb!' Jake said gloomily, throwing himself down into a leather couch and tearing off the string and brown paper. A few seconds later he was staring at an exquisitely small, Rockingham china model of a castle. Attached to it was a label which read: *'The rich man in his castle, the poor man at his gate, but who'll care for poor old Elsie when she's homeless—it will be too late.'*

Jake looked around the large room which was now mercifully silent; at the cloth-covered birdcages and the baskets, whose feline inhabitants had temporarily suspended their caterwauling to drink the milk which Carter had found for them. He was suddenly struck by the whole, ridiculous aspect of an apartment that had been, up to an hour ago, the pride and joy of an expensive interior decorator, but which now looked more like feeding time at the zoo!

He gave a brief snort of grim amusement and removed a small note pad from his wallet. Buried deep in thought, twisting it idly back and forth in his fingers for a few minutes, he finally gave a heavy sigh, shaking his head at his own folly as he reached for the 'phone.

CHAPTER FIVE

HARRIET remained standing where she was for some time after Jake had stormed out of the flat, slamming the door so hard behind his departing figure that it had shaken the old building. Dry-eyed and exhausted, she eventually pulled herself together and trailed slowly around the room, picking up the empty glasses and taking them through to the kitchen before going out into the little paved garden.

Sitting curled up on the plump cushions of a wide bench seat, with Montmorency draped across her lap, she listened to the muted sounds of traffic, and the distant noise of people walking by on the street outside. It was a lovely, warm, dusky evening, and like the moths fluttering helplessly around the patio light, so her own chaotic, agitated thoughts whirled in flustered confusion.

It had seemed a very simple, straightforward matter just over two weeks ago, when she and her friends had met to plan their demonstration outside the headquarters of Lancaster International. There had been no question in anyone's mind, let alone hers, that Jason Lancaster was a prime example of a hard-nosed, ruthless capitalist determinedly grinding the faces of the poor—in this particular instance, that of Mrs Elsie Peters. It was a very clear-cut, classic case, and one about which she had possessed not the slightest twinge of doubt.

So far, so good—or bad—depending on one's point of view. If she had been writing a legal appraisal of the case, Harriet could have laid it out in clear, precise and

Win "Instantly" right now in another way

...try our Preview Service

Get **4** **FREE** full-length Harlequin Presents® books

Plus this elegant jewelry bag

Plus a surprise free gift

Plus lots more!

Our love stories are popular everywhere...and WE'RE CELE-BRATING with free birthday prizes—free gifts—and a fabulous no-strings offer.

Simply try our Preview Service. With your trial, you get SNEAK PREVIEW RIGHTS to eight new HARLEQUIN PRESENTS novels a month—months before they are in stores—with 10%-OFF retail on any books you keep (just $1.75 each)—and Free Home Delivery besides.

THERE IS NO CATCH. You're not required to buy a single book, ever. You may even cancel Preview Service privileges anytime, if you want. The free gifts are yours anyway, as tokens of our appreciation.

It's a super sweet deal if ever there was one. Try us and see.

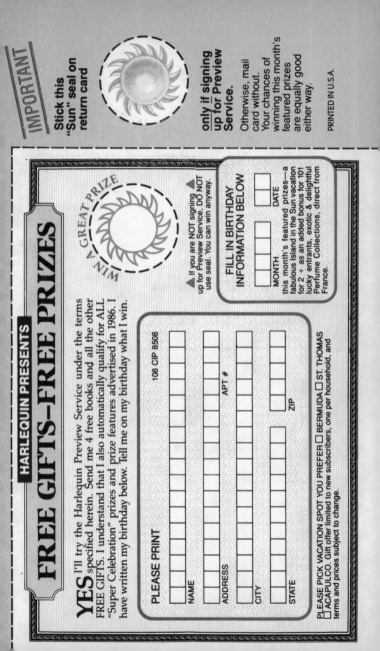

HARLEQUIN PRESENTS

FREE GIFTS–FREE PRIZES

YES I'll try the Harlequin Preview Service under the terms specified herein. Send me 4 free books and all the other FREE GIFTS. I understand that I also automatically qualify for ALL "Super Celebration" prizes and prize features advertised in 1986. I have written my birthday below. Tell me on my birthday what I win.

WIN A GREAT PRIZE

▲ If you are NOT signing up for Preview Service. DO NOT use seal. You can win anyway.

FILL IN BIRTHDAY INFORMATION BELOW

| MONTH | | DATE |

this month's featured prizes—a fabulous Island in the Sun vacation for 2 + as an added bonus for 101 lucky entrants, exotic & delightful Perfume Collections, direct from France.

PLEASE PRINT

108 CIP 8508

NAME

ADDRESS   APT #

CITY

STATE   ZIP

PLEASE PICK VACATION SPOT YOU PREFER ☐ BERMUDA ☐ ST. THOMAS ☐ ACAPULCO. Gift offer limited to new subscribers, one per household, and terms and prices subject to change.

Harlequin
"Super Celebration" Sweepstakes
901 Fuhrmann Blvd.
P.O. Box 1867
Buffalo, NY 14240-1867

PLACE
1ST CLASS
STAMP
HERE

logical terms. Unfortunately, there appeared to be
nothing clear or logical regarding her feelings about
Jake Lancaster.

After the confrontation in his office, Harriet had
become aware that while Jake was undeniably a tough,
ruthless businessman, he was not entirely without a
social conscience. She had discovered that what had at
first appeared to be so very black and white had turned
out, like most things in life, to be composed of varying
shades of grey. So that when he had confessed that he
knew nothing of his subsidiary company's iniquitous
behaviour, and promised that he would sort out the
matter—she had believed him. Maybe, like
Montmorency, she was a very bad judge of character,
but she had been totally convinced that when Jake said
he would do something, he did it. That was obviously
why she had felt so let down these past two weeks, and
which had added fuel to the flames of her anger,
resulting in her plan of retaliation and retribution.

Trying to rationalise her own reactions to the affair
in which she had become embroiled was proving to be a
hard, if not impossible task. Just as difficult as it was to
prevent her mind filling with visions of Jake. Every
expression on his hard face, all that he had said and
done that day, seemed to be etched on her brain.
Especially the turbulent effect on her emotions when
she had found herself clasped so tightly in his arms . . .

'I've got to pull myself together!' she told
Montmorency firmly, giving him a quick hug before
uncurling her long legs and rising to her feet.
Wandering aimlessly around the garden as she tried to
ignore a strange, persistent ache inside her, Harriet
eventually decided to seek the comforting solace of a
hot bath.

Lying in the warm scented water, she tried to bring
some order to bear upon her confused emotions. Jake

had walked out of her life and, of course, it was right that he should have done so, she told herself sternly. Nothing could possibly come of the strong, almost overwhelming attraction that drew her to him. Not when they were such very different people, and he was already engaged to marry another woman. Even thinking about him was pointless. It was too late. There wasn't anything she could do to halt the plan she had put into operation, which had been conceived when she thought he had deliberately ignored the case of old Mrs Peters. The fact that it had been a genuine mis-understanding on her part wasn't going to cut any ice with Jake. Not when he was faced with all those birds and cats, nor the other items with which she had embellished the scheme. He had gone out of her life forever, and she must just accept the fact and think of something else very, very quickly . . .

Attempting to empty her mind of Jake's disturbing personality, Harriet tried to concentrate on more mundane matters as she stepped out of the bath. It wasn't as if she didn't have a thousand and one things she ought to be doing. Items such as taking Montmorency for a walk, sweeping and dusting the flat, and defrosting the fridge which seemed to ice up so quickly in this hot weather.

A quick ring on the door bell made her heart leap into her throat for a moment. She wasn't entirely sure who she expected to find on the doorstep, but she was ashamed at her deep sense of disappointment to find that it was only Rosie.

'Come on in. Sorry about this,' she murmured, clutching the towel about her tall figure. 'I've just been having a bath, but it won't take me a minute to sling some clothes on.'

'There's no hurry, just as long as I'm not holding you up, or anything.'

'No, of course you're not. Fix yourself a drink or some coffee, and I'll be back in a minute.'

Escaping to her bedroom, Harriet was horrified to see the dark circles under her wide grey eyes. Clearly the result of all those stupid tears earlier. Grimacing at her reflection, she climbed into a faded pair of jeans and a loose shirt before hunting through her make-up box for some camouflage. Since she hardly ever wore any cosmetics, there wasn't much she could find, finally settling for some blusher to disguise her pale cheeks and a coral pink lipstick to draw attention away from her eyes. Maybe Rosie wouldn't notice anything amiss.

Rosie did notice. 'You look terrible. Are you feeling all right, Harry?'

'It's been a long day, so I expect I'm just tired, that's all.'

'Hmm.' The small blonde girl looked thoughtfully at her friend, but decided to say no more on the subject. 'I really just popped in for two things. Firstly, I hope you haven't forgotten that you promised to make me one of your yummy, scrummy chocolate cakes for tea this Sunday?'

'Oh, Lord—yes I had!' Harriet gave her a guilty smile. 'Still, it's only Friday, so there's no need to panic. Who are you trying to impress this time?'

'Well, there's this really handsome hulk of a guy I met while I was working part-time in the local pub last week. I could tell he fancied me rotten,' she grinned. 'The only trouble is that he's looking for a girl who can cook like his mother!'

Harriet couldn't help laughing at the idea of Rosie, whose love life was extensive and chaotic, trying to pretend to be a little homebody. 'You idiot! You can't even boil an egg. I don't think this new romance sounds as if it's even going to get off the ground!'

'You leave me to worry about that!' her friend

grinned. 'I reckon one slice of your chocky cake—and I'll have him off the ground and into bed before you can say, "mummy's boy"!'

Harriet tried not to look shocked. What Rosie did was her own business, she told herself firmly. And anyway, she was hardly in a position to take a high moral tone about other people's behaviour. Not when, only an hour ago, she herself had been involved in a fairly torrid, passionate scene on that sofa over there— and with a man whom she barely knew!

'Hey, are you sure you're feeling okay?' Rosie looked with concern at the tall girl's flushed face. 'You've probably been overdoing it at that law centre ... oh, that's the other thing I meant to ask you. How's the scheme to punish that sexy Jake Lancaster coming along?'

'I—um—I really don't know,' Harriet muttered, turning away to pour herself a glass of wine. 'After our discussion the other night, I arranged for everything to be delivered, but I haven't heard ... well, I mean, I don't know exactly how ... Oh—!' she swore angrily. 'I've spilt my wine.'

Rosie raised her eyebrows in astonishment. She was very fond of Harry, who was one of the kindest girls she knew, even if she was pretty square and old-fashioned. She'd certainly never heard her friend use bad language before—so what had got into her now? And why swear about something as minor as a little spilt wine? 'What's wrong, Harry?' she asked quietly. 'If there's anything I can do ...' Her words were interrupted by the loud ringing of the telephone.

Harriet spun around, staring at the instrument in horror. Was it ...? No it couldn't possibly be ...?

'Aren't you going to answer it?' Rosie looked at her in puzzlement, her blue eyes widening as she caught

sight of the hectic flushed cheeks and trembling hands of the girl across the room.

'Yes, I—I suppose I'd better,' Harriet mumbled, trying to pull her shattered nerves together as she picked up the receiver.

'Er . . . hello?'

'Harriet?' There was no mistaking those deep rich tones, nor the American accent.

Her heart pounded. 'Yes,' she murmured, wishing she was dead.

'I just thought you'd be pleased to know that all the birds, cats, heaters and flowers have duly arrived,' Jake purred menacingly. 'Oh, I mustn't forget to mention the cases of something called "stout", which my man, Carter, tells me is very good to drink with champagne. Know anything about that particular fetish?'

'I—er—I think it's called "black velvet",' she replied without thinking, and then realised that he wasn't shouting or raging at her, as she had fully expected him to do. 'I know it's much too late, but I am truly, truly sorry about—well, about everything,' she added quickly, bracing herself for the blast to come.

'Hmm. Well, I might—just might, mind you!— decided not to throttle you to death. But that decision will depend upon you contacting the people who delivered all these delightful surprises, *and get them out of my apartment—immediately!*'

She gulped nervously. 'Oh dear! I'm—er—terribly sorry, but I honestly don't think I can. Not tonight, anyway.'

'*Dear God!*' Jake groaned, and she held her breath fearing the worst. 'Okay, Harriet,' he said after a long pause. 'I've decided that what we're going to have, is a trade off.'

'A—a what?'

'I want you to guarantee to have everything out of

my apartment by lunchtime tomorrow. In return, and providing there are no stray birds or any of those damn screeching cats left lying about, I will pick you up at ten o'clock sharp on Sunday morning.'

Her lips felt suddenly dry. 'Why? I mean—whatever for?' she asked breathlessly.

'To go and see Mrs Elsie Peters, of course. Oh, by the way, Harriet,' he added softly. 'The next time you feel the urge to write some poetry—do try and make sure that the last line scans properly, hmm?'

The sound of his low, sardonic laughter was abruptly silenced as he rang off. Harriet was shaking like a leaf as she replaced her own receiver, and she stood staring blankly into space for a moment, until recalled to the present by Rosie's voice.

'Goodness—who was that? You looked frightened to death!'

'Yes, well, I think I could do with a drink,' Harriet muttered, filling up both their glasses. Really, she thought, bemusedly viewing the empty wine bottle, that was about the third or fourth glass of wine she'd had today, which was about the same amount as she normally drank in a week. If she went on like this she would undoubtedly become a dipsomaniac!

'Come on, Harry—spill the beans!' Rosie urged. 'I know I'm being thoroughly nosy, but I'm dying to know about your mysterious caller. He or she certainly had you in a flap!'

'It—it was Jake Lancaster.'

'Wow! No wonder you looked as if you expected to be struck by lightning any minute. Was he simply furious about all those budgerigars? Serve the horrid man right!

'No, well, it isn't as simple as that ...' Harriet hesitated, and then began to explain how Jake had come off the plane to pick her up at the law centre,

taken her back to the flat, and his explanation of why nothing had been done about the case of Mrs Peters. 'He could possibly be lying, Rosie, but I'm sure he's not. When he outlined his movements, I could see that he really hadn't a spare moment in which to look into the matter. I—well, I felt awful! There were all those things arriving at his apartment, and there was nothing I could do to stop them.'

'He'll live!' Rosie said brutally. 'Anyway, I shouldn't think an experience like that will do the glamorous Mr Lancaster any harm at all. In fact, it will undoubtedly do him a great deal of good to spend a night with all those birds and cats!' she giggled. 'I wish I was a fly on his apartment wall—I should think it's bedlam, don't you?' she added, collapsing on to a chair and roaring with laughter.

Harriet tried to see the amusing side of the débâcle, but she seemed to have temporarily lost her sense of humour. 'You can laugh,' she said to her friend. 'But he's going to kill me if I don't get everything out of his apartment by tomorrow afternoon. Since that'll mean spending the morning on the 'phone, you can just about wave goodbye to your chocolate cake.'

'Oh, come on, Harry—for heaven's sake don't be so gloomy. I'll help you with the telephone calls.' She paused, gazing at Harriet's worried expression, and the wine sloshing about the glass held in her nervously trembling hands. 'You really do care, don't you?' she said slowly. 'That was why you were in such a state earlier on. And now I come to think of it—why did Jake Lancaster go to the law centre, and then drive you back here? He hasn't ...? You don't really ...? Oh, my goodness!' Rosie exclaimed as a deep flush spread over her friend's face. 'You two are having it off together!'

'No—of course we're not!' Harriet snapped. 'It—it's

nothing like that! I—er—I just felt sorry that I'd misjudged him, that's all.'

'Oh, yes?' Rosie grinned. 'Are you seriously trying to tell me that Jake Lancaster came straight off the plane from Hong Kong, after about an eighteen hour flight, and didn't return to his apartment, but immediately sought you out at the law centre—just to discuss Mrs Peters? Do me a favour, Harry! That's the most ridiculous thing I've heard in a long time.'

'But I promise you, that's exactly what happened,' Harriet assured her earnestly.

Her friend laughed. 'Honestly—you're as green as grass! Of course I believe that's what happened. But it's straining even my credulity too far, to expect me to believe that sexy Jake had Mrs Peters on his mind. If he'd felt that strongly, he could have 'phoned you, couldn't he?'

'Yes, well, I suppose he did mention something about dinner . . .' Harriet mumbled.

'*Ah ha!*'

'Oh, why don't you shut up, Rosie? I promise you that there's nothing going on. All I know is that I'm feeling very tired, and completely fed up with the whole business!' At least that last statement's true, Harriet told herself, realising that she was just about ready to drop with nervous exhaustion and fatigue.

'Okay, okay. There's no need to snap.'

'I'm sorry. I . . .'

'That's all right, Harry. I should mind my own damn business. But at the risk of getting my head bitten off again, please do be careful, won't you? Jake Lancaster may be ultra glamorous, rich and handsome, and just about everything else you can think of, but don't forget I got a good look at him outside his offices on the day of the demonstration. Believe me, he's also a *very* tough, hard and ruthless man.' She looked at Harriet with concern.

'I've knocked around a lot more than you have, love, and believe me—guys like that are apt to eat innocent young girls like you for breakfast, and then speedily disappear to search for another tasty morsel! And they nearly always have the safety net of an understanding wife—or in Jake's case, a fiancée—tucked away in the background. So, do realise that you're playing with fire, and take care not to get burnt, okay?'

Lying in bed later that night, wide awake and unable to sleep despite being so tired, Harriet thought about Rosie's words. Maybe she was, as her friend had said, 'green as grass'. She had never, in fact, been much of a romantic, and had always considered herself too sensible and level-headed to lose any sleep over a man. Having seen some of her friends battered by storms of passion, generally over the most unsuitable and unreliable boyfriends, she had thanked her lucky stars that such mental and physical disruption wasn't for her. There had only been one occasion when she had fallen head over heels in love. And she now saw that it had only been a temporary infatuation, swiftly killed by the discovery that the man had been interested solely in her money. After that . . . well, it had seemed easier to give her love and affection to the people who didn't have her advantages in life, or to her pets who demanded nothing from her and yet who returned her loving care with their devotion. That way, life was much safer, somehow.

Tossing restlessly, Harriet threw back the covers. It was such a hot night, no wonder she couldn't sleep. Maybe she should get up, make a cup of tea and cook that damn chocolate cake? She smiled wryly at the thought of herself padding around in the kitchen in the early hours of the morning, and of Rosie's conviction that one slice of the cake would prove to be a powerful aphrodisiac! Goodness knows what was going to

happen at her friend's tea party on Sunday, but that was one relationship that was clearly doomed from the start.

She sighed heavily. Thinking about the subject of doomed relationships, led her straight back to Jake. It was clearly no good trying to hide her head in the sand. Jake's strong, magnetic personality was filling her mind to the exclusion of all else, just as he had monopolised most of her waking moments and her dreams for the past two weeks. She might as well squarely face up to the fact that when he had slammed the door behind him, it was a symbolic gesture that signalled the death knell of their relationship. It had been so brief that maybe—well, almost certainly, if she was going to be honest—it never had a chance from the very start. After all, there couldn't be many romances that had begun with an angry shouting match on a city pavement, and which had proceeded to go rapidly downhill ever since. Even if he had been terribly kind and comforting when she had been so upset about Mrs O'Casey, it didn't really mean anything significant. Feeling compassion and giving good advice to a woman who had stupidly tried to cope with something that was way beyond her, wasn't that unusual—even for a high-powered businessman. And why she was thinking about her turbulent relationship with Jake in terms of 'a romance' she had no idea. He had only kissed her twice, and he would hardly regard that as a big deal. As Rosie had so graphically pointed out, he was an experienced man of the world, undoubtedly given to picking up and discarding women without a moment's thought. And there could be few women who, given half a chance, wouldn't leap at it—and into his bed! Even she, pathetically inexperienced as she was, could see just what a devastating lover he would be.

Trembling as she remembered the wave of sensual excitement she had felt in his arms, Harriet rolled over and buried her face in the pillow. She must—she simply must stop thinking about that brief episode. She would be seeing Jake for only one more time, when she took him to see Mrs Peters on Sunday, and she must make sure that she was cool, calm and collected. Because Rosie's advice had been absolutely right. Having anything at all to do with Jake Lancaster, was like playing with fire. If she didn't want to get burnt, she must quickly dowse the flickering flames of what could only be a hopeless infatuation.

Harriet woke up on Sunday morning and gave a yelp of dismay as she looked at her bedside clock. Goodness knows she had been tired after hectically speeding around London all yesterday, but how could she have been so stupid as to forget to set her alarm? Jumping out of bed, she rushed feverishly around the flat, ruthlessly ignoring Montmorency's unhappy whine as she lifted him into the bathtub.

'It's no good howling at me like that. Your coat's an absolute disgrace—all dirty and matted—we can't possibly let Mrs Peters see you in that filthy condition!' she panted, trying to steady the wriggling dog with one hand, while she worked in the shampoo with another. 'And if you must go and dig up half the garden, on the one day when I need lots of time in which to make sure that I'm as cool, calm and collected as possible—then all I can say is, you deserve all you're getting, you beastly animal!'

Towelling him dry as quickly as she could, Harriet scampered through the rest of the chores before hurrying into her bedroom. What on earth was she going to wear? That damned man was bound to arrive absolutely on the dot of ten o'clock, and with only

twenty minutes to go she didn't have a hope of being ready on time.

Jake was as punctual as she had instinctively known he would be. His tanned face expressionless and giving nothing away as she opened the door to his knock. Only his blue eyes, gleaming as they viewed her tall figure, seemed to display any life at all. Leaning nonchalantly against the architrave of the open door, his gaze moved slowly over the thick cloud of her chestnut hair and on down over the full skirted, buttercup-yellow sleeveless dress. It was like being under a microscope, and she didn't care for the sensation. Harriet's lips tightened in annoyance. Well, if he thought she looked 'crazy' or 'bizarre', which appeared to be two of his favourite adjectives, then it was just too bad! If he did but know it, the dress was one that Aunt Clarissa had bullied her into buying—at Harrods, naturally!—and it had seemed eminently suitable to wear on this visit to Mrs Peters. It was only now, beneath his intense scrutiny, that she began to wonder if the tightly fitted bodice with its scooped neckline wasn't perhaps a little too revealing?

'Isn't it time we left?' she asked, irritated to note the slight breathlessness in her voice.

'If you insist,' Jake murmured with a grin. Leading the way down the steps, he opened the passenger door of his black sports car and turned to face her, his dark eyebrows arching in surprise as he noticed the dog at her heels. 'I didn't realise that I was to have the honour of chauffeuring Montmorency!'

Harriet wished she could swipe that grin off his face. I've got to have someone on my side of the fence—I can't cope with you on my own! she wanted to shout at the tough, formidable man. But she managed a casual shrug as she closed the front door behind her and

walked slowly towards him. 'It will be a treat for him. Mrs Peters is very fond of dogs,' she said, bending down to pat Montmorency's head.

'Hmm. It sounds more like a case of: "where I go, my dog goes too".'

The damn man's too perceptive by half! Harriet thought, catching the dry note of amusement in his voice. Raising her head, her cheeks flushed as she saw the sardonic gleam in his brilliant blue eyes.

'Okay, Montmorency, in you get,' Jake said, pushing the passenger seat forward, enabling the shaggy dog to leap into the back of the vehicle. 'God knows, I've met some chaperones in my time, but let's face it, old boy—you certainly are different!' he added with a brief laugh.

They had been travelling through the streets for some moments, before Jake turned to glance at the woman sitting silently beside him. 'I haven't said how much I deeply appreciate the fact that my apartment is no longer filled to the brim with all those cats and birds.'

So he should be! she thought, wincing at the heavy irony in his voice as she stared down at the hands clenched tightly together in her lap. Having spent all yesterday morning on the 'phone contacting the various suppliers of the animals and objects she had sent to his apartment, Harriet had been frankly exhausted. Even if it hadn't backfired so disastrously, she would have heartily regretted ever having thought of the damn scheme. Why on earth hadn't she realised that it was one thing to order various articles, and quite another to persuade the suppliers to take them back? Some of the shopkeepers had proved to be extremely rude and abusive,

'Yes, well, I really am very, very sorry,' she muttered.

'So was I!' he said grimly. 'If I hadn't managed to get hold of you that evening, I can promise you, my dear

Harriet, that I would have personally beaten the living daylights out of you the next morning!'

Harriet gritted her teeth. She was sick and tired of the whole beastly subject. She'd said she was sorry—which she was—and she was damned if she was going to keep on apologising all day. Besides, she was far more interested in hearing the answer to a question that had been troubling her. 'How did you know my telephone number?' she asked, and then wished she hadn't as she saw his lips twitch with amusement.

'It was no great feat of deduction. I merely made a note of it when I was in your apartment.'

She ought to have guessed that's what he'd done. His address book was probably filled to the brim with strange girls' telephone numbers, she thought gloomily, stealing a glance through her eyelashes at the tanned, hard profile of the man who sat beside her. He always looked immaculate, and today was no exception even if he was far more casually dressed than normal. Clothed in slim navy blue trousers, topped by a short-sleeved white shirt open at the neck to display the strong tanned column of his throat, Jake exuded such an air of raw, vibrant masculinity that she was finding it difficult to concentrate on the reason for their visit to Mrs Peters.

'. . . wake up, Harriet!' his voice interrupted her confused thoughts. 'You haven't told me exactly where the old lady lives.'

She gave him the direction, and then prompted by some evil demon, she added smugly, 'It wasn't a very bright idea of yours to drive here in this glamorous car. In this sort of neighbourhood, you've only to turn your back to find all the wheels have disappeared—if not the whole vehicle!'

'I'm touched by your concern,' he said gravely as he drew the car to a halt. Switching off the engine, he got

out and beckoned to a teenaged boy leaning against a nearby wall.

'What did you say to him?' she asked as Jake opened her door and Montmorency bounded past her into the street.

'I hope you're not *too* disappointed, Harriet! I promised the boy a large tip if he made sure no one laid their sticky fingers on the Ferrari.' He smiled lazily down into her eyes, and she could willingly have hit him. 'It was sweet of you to warn me, but I never leave anything to chance.'

'I must try and remember that little nugget of fascinating information,' she murmured sarcastically, before whistling to Montmorency and walking across the road to Mrs Peters' door. She was never going to get the better of that hard, ruthless man, she thought despondently as she waited for the old lady to answer her knock. And as for this visit—it was sure to be nothing more or less than a complete disaster.

However, almost two hours later, when Jake was ushering her and the dog back into the car, she was forced to admit to herself that she couldn't have been more wrong. Harriet had thought hard and long, yesterday, about whether she should prepare Mrs Peters for Jake's presence, and had decided on balance that it was better if the old lady wasn't given too much time in which to worry about his proposed visit. And her decision not to mention that she was bringing the dreaded Mr Lancaster had proved to be the right one. Mrs Peters had been initially flustered by his presence, but had soon succumbed to Jake's warm charm. And he hadn't been feigning an interest in the elderly woman's problems. Harriet had been sceptical at first, but it was obvious that not only had he done his homework on the proposed development, and was fully conversant with the layout of the area,

but he was genuinely interested in hearing what Mrs Peters had to say.

Harriet was still buried in thought, trying to come to terms with this new and surprising aspect of Jake's character, when she realised that she had been sitting in the car for some considerable time. Looking up, she was shocked to find that they appeared to be travelling across a bridge over the river Thames.

'Where on earth are we going?' she demanded.

'To my house in Sussex,' he said calmly. 'Surely you haven't forgotten our bargain? You promised to clear all those creatures out of my apartment,' he added as she looked at him in confusion, 'and in return I agreed to take you out today.'

'But only to see Mrs Peters,' she said accusingly.

'Didn't I tell you that I'd arranged for us to have lunch and spend the rest of the day at my home in Sussex?' He shook his head in mock sorrow. 'Dear me, I don't know how I came to forget that. Never mind. Just think how much Montmorency will enjoy himself running about the countryside, hmm?'

'This is the third time you've practically abducted me—and I won't have it!' she protested angrily.

'Oh, come on Harriet! There's no need to get so excited. Why don't you just relax and . . .'

'Nuts to you! And don't bother turning on all that smooth charm of yours—it may be a heavy number with your fiancée, or old Mrs Peters, but it doesn't impress me one little bit!' She shouted, overcome by fury at his high-handed behaviour. 'Let me tell you, Mr Jason Lancaster—*oh . . .!*'

Harriet had been so busy giving vent to her outraged feelings, she hadn't noticed that Jake had pulled into the side of the road. He swiftly cut the engine and released their seat-belts, and before she knew what was happening she suddenly found herself jerked forward

and crushed in his powerful embrace. Harriet tried to catch her breath, but the mouth that seized her parted lips was firm and determined, his arms moulding her slim body to the hard strength of his muscular chest. Quivering uncontrollably, she was almost faint with dizziness, when his lips softened and he began a slow, sensual invasion of the inner softness of her mouth that totally and finally sapped what was left of her strength. No one, except this man, had ever kissed her in such an erotic and sexual way and she moaned helplessly, swept by a wanton desire to respond and surrender as the effect of his deepening kiss possessed her trembling body.

An age seemed to pass before he raised his dark head to look down at the girl lying exhausted in his arms. 'Experience of life has taught me that there is only one certain way to silence a woman, and that is to kiss her! And in your case, Harriet, it was a delightful pleasure to do so!' he murmured softly, removing his hard arms from about her trembling figure and settling her back in her own seat.

'You got on your high horse so quickly just now, that you didn't give me a chance to say that far from abducting you, I merely wished us to spend a pleasant day in the country,' he continued quietly. 'However, if you insist on my taking you back to your apartment, which can only be very hot and sticky on such a warm day as this—I will, of course, do so. But wouldn't you really prefer to enjoy the cool, fresh air of the countryside?'

Harriet tried to collect her scattered wits. Jake was right. Quite apart from her own, very mixed emotional feelings about the man sitting beside her, she would love to get away from the heat and dust of the city. But she couldn't possibly agree to his suggestion—not when she had nailed her colours so firmly to the mast. She

despised herself for being so concerned with saving face, but she had somehow got herself into an impossible situation from which she couldn't see how to extract herself.

Jake's voice cut into the strained silence. 'I really think you ought to force yourself to cast aside your anger with me, and concentrate on what is best for old Montmorency. London, in the summer and without a park nearby, isn't much fun for dogs and I'm sure he ought to have a day out chasing rabbits, or whatever. You'd enjoy that, wouldn't you?' he added, turning his head to address the large English sheepdog panting happily in the back seat of the car. 'Yes, I thought so. Montmorency says that he agrees with me, so it looks as if you're outvoted two to one, Harriet!'

'You are a quite incorrigible man! Do you always treat women like this?' she asked sternly, trying not to respond to Jake's infectious grin.

'You could reasonably be forgiven for thinking so, but strangely enough, I don't,' he said seriously as the smile died on his lips. There was a long pause while he stared out of the window, his face stern and impassive and then he gave a light sigh. 'Okay, how about if I apologise for my behaviour, and faithfully promise that we shall have a peaceful and uncomplicated day from now on, hmm?'

'Well . . .' Harriet hesitated. 'How about—I mean, is your fiancée going to be there too?'

'My fiancée flew off to Brazil on a modelling assignment, yesterday evening,' he said in a bland, toneless voice. 'Magda is, quite rightly, very angry with me for being rude to her on the telephone. And the reason I was so discourteous, is *solely* due to the fact that when she rang, I was in a thoroughly bad temper trying to cope with all those delightful little surprises you had laid on in my apartment.'

'Oh . . . oh dear.'

'Oh, dear, indeed—you wretched girl!' Jake gave a harsh, dry bark of laughter. 'I think it might be a good idea, under the circumstances, if we changed the subject, or I might be tempted to revert to my original idea of throttling you to death!' He started the engine of the car. 'Okay, what's it to be, London or Sussex?'

His voice sounded casual, but she knew that he wasn't quite sure of her answer because she felt his intense gaze on her averted face.

'Montmorency seems to have the casting vote, so I suppose we'd better go down to Sussex,' she said as calmly as she could, avoiding his eyes as she settled back in her seat. While the black Ferrari roared down the motorway, Harriet tried to come to terms with her emotional response to his mind-shattering kiss. Every time she found herself in his company or in his arms, she seemed to go completely to pieces. She couldn't really be falling in love with him, could she? A man she hardly knew? The whole idea was quite ridiculous! And so was she for having such an overheated imagination.

Just before they reached Midhurst, Jake turned off on to a narrow road which meandered away across the Sussex downs. The air through her open window smelt deliciously fresh, fragrant with the smell of new-mown hay and the flowers growing in the cottage gardens. It really was a perfect summer's day, and Harriet realised that in opting for a day in the country, she had made the right decision. There was absolutely no doubt, of course, that she ought to be feeling deeply ashamed of having caused so much trouble between Jake and his fiancée, but she couldn't help feeling suddenly very cheerful and quite extraordinarily light-hearted.

CHAPTER SIX

DURING the journey, Harriet had amused herself by speculating about the sort of house that Jake might be likely to own, but hadn't come to a final conclusion as to what to expect when, after driving through country lanes for some time, he slowed down and turned off the road. Passing through a wide entrance, set with grey stone pillars bearing massive wrought iron gates, they sped down a long gravelled drive bordered on either side by copper beech trees, coming to a halt in front of a large Tudor manor house, covered in ivy and rambling yellow roses.

She gazed with delight at the many gables, the tall Elizabethan chimneys and the lead-lined, mullioned windows sparkling in the sun. 'It's lovely!' she exclaimed as Jake came around to help her and Montmorency to alight from the car.

'Dragons looks its best at this time of year,' he agreed.

'What an unusual name for a house. Is it Saxon?'

Jake laughed. 'I can hardly bear to tell you, since it will undoubtedly reinforce all your dark suspicions about me. However, the real name of this place is Dragon's Lair—and where that originated from, I have no idea.'

'You are right, it is an extremely apt name for your house!' She gave him a mocking grin as he led her towards a large oak door, which was opened by a grey haired man, dressed in a white linen jacket and dark trousers.

'Ah, I don't think you two have met each other. Carter, this 'is Miss Harriet Drummond, about

whom you may have heard me speak in extremely harsh accents. However, it is far too nice a day to quarrel, and so I have decided to forget temporarily what happened last Friday.'

'Quite right, sir. One of my late gentlemen, a man renowned for his good works, always said that magnanimity was one of the cardinal virtues.'

Harriet stared down at the stone flagged floor of the large hall, her face flaming with embarrassment, but as Montmorency jerked at his lead, she raised her eyes to see that despite his sepulchral tones, Carter's eyes were twinkling with amusement.

'Mrs Benson has carried out your orders regarding luncheon,' he told Jake before turning to Harriet. 'I imagine that your dog must be thirsty after the journey. Would he care for a drink of water?'

'Yes, please,' she answered, giving Jake a quick smile before following the manservant out of the hall and on down a long corridor.

'I—er—I have told Mr Lancaster that I'm sorry about—well, about sending all those things to his apartment. But I suppose that I really ought to apologise to you as well,' she said as they stood in the kitchen while Montmorency quenched his thirst.

'It was somewhat trying at the time, Miss, but I can assure you that I have quite forgotten the episode, as I am sure Mr Lancaster will also do so before very long.'

'No, I think that's probably expecting too much!' Harriet laughed, looking around the large room. It was equipped with all the modern aids to cookery, but it possessed the warm, homely air of a farmhouse kitchen.

'The housekeeper, Mrs Benson, has provided a large bone for your dog. It was thought that the animal might like to eat it in the kitchen garden, where Benson—who also oversees the garden as well as

chauffeuring Mr Lancaster—is, I understand, busy hoeing his carrots.'

Harriet smiled, at Carter's prissy tones, and at the thought of the treat for her dog. 'Montmorency will be delighted to accept the invitation,' she said gravely. 'Although, do please ask Benson *not* to let him bury the bone—I've had to bath the horrid animal once already today!'

'Pardon me for asking,' Carter coughed delicately as Montmorency finished drinking his water and began exploring the kitchen. 'But I have been wondering if, by any chance, you might be the late John Drummond's daughter? I used to care for a gentleman who worked in the City, and he was a great friend of both Mr Drummond and his brother-in-law, Sir Ralph Worthington. Many's the time . . .' he paused, looking with concern at Harriet's pale face. 'Are you feeling all right, Miss?'

'Yes, I—I'm fine.' Harriet took a deep breath. 'You're quite correct, John Drummond was my father. But . . . well, to tell you the truth, Carter, your employer doesn't know anything about my family background. It's . . . um . . . rather difficult and . . . and far too complicated to explain exactly why I haven't told him. However,' she added quickly, 'I would be *most* grateful if you wouldn't mind keeping that information strictly to yourself.'

'Say no more, Miss Drummond!' The elderly man beamed at her, one of his eyelids closing with the faintest suggestion of a wink. 'I can well understand that there comes a certain stage in a romance, when a slight air of mystery can do nothing but—er—enhance the affair.'

Harriet frowned in puzzlement. What on earth was the man talking about? 'I really don't think . . .'

'Say no more, Miss Drummond. You may rely on my

lips remaining sealed on the matter,' he assured her gravely. 'And now, perhaps you would like to wash your hands before joining Mr Lancaster in the drawing room?'

Walking slowly back into the square panelled hall, Harriet tried to ignore the apprehensive feeling that was gnawing away inside her. Could she rely on Carter keeping quiet about her father? She could only hope and pray that he would, although she was well aware that there was no class of people more snobbish or given to gossip, than old family retainers. Carter seemed to be a bit dotty around the edges—what was all that nonsense about romance and mystery?—and if he was going to spill the beans, then there was likely to be an almighty row. Jake appeared to have forgotten that she held a fair number of shares in his company, and he wasn't going to be best pleased if and when he discovered that she wasn't entirely what he supposed her to be. Maybe she ought to try and find an opportunity to tell him, herself? It wasn't anything particularly dramatic, after all, and the likelihood of his rushing off to tell Aunt Clarissa all about Harriet's two separate lifestyles, was practically nil.

She bent down to bury her nose in a bowl of yellow roses, before walking over to run her fingers over the old oak panelling, whose rich patina was clearly the result of many years loving attention. The wide oak staircase was equally old, its carved newel post illuminated by the sunlight pouring in from a large mullioned window.

'Ah, there you are!' Jake strode into the hall and took her arm, ushering her through another large panelled room decorated in warm, earthy colours, and on out to a wide stone terrace. 'How about a glass of champagne before lunch? Although, if you want—what did you call

it ... a "black velvet"?—then I'm afraid that we no longer have any stout!'

'You're never going to let me forget that, are you?' she grinned in response to his teasing smile.

'Who knows? Anything is possible, although I fear that I will always shudder when I see a budgerigar or a Siamese cat!' His eyes were gleaming with sardonic amusement as he handed her a tall fluted glass. Do you like my house?' he asked, leading her over to sit down on the low stone wall of the terrace.

'Very much. It's so lovely and peaceful.' Harriet looked around at the clumps of mature trees grouped about the landscaped park surrounding the house, and at the lush green lawns which ran down to what looked like an ornamental lake in the distance. 'It must be centuries old.'

Jake smiled. 'I hope you won't be disappointed if I tell you that while it does rest on the medieval foundations of an old barn, the house itself was only built at the turn of the century. The panelling and staircase are, of course, very old. I believe they were taken from some mansion that was being demolished when this house was built.'

'I'd never have guessed it,' she mused, turning to look at the ancient-looking, grey stone walls. 'Have you lived here long?'

'No—I only bought it about four years ago for my mother who lives in America. Although it was designed by Sir Edward Lutyens for a wealthy shipping family, it had been let go to rack and ruin. By the time I had restored it to its former glory, my dear mother had changed her mind about coming to live over here in Britain!' He smiled and shrugged his shoulders. 'I expect she decided to stay in America to be near my sister and her grandchildren.'

'What a pity.' And then, prompted by her evil genius,

she added, 'This is obviously a family house. Are you
and Magda planning to have lots of children?'

Oh, Lord! she thought as his expression became
suddenly harsh and forbidding. Why on earth couldn't
she keep her mouth shut? Harriet buried her nose in the
rising bubbles of the champagne in her glass, nervously
aware of his eyes on her flushed face.

Much to her relief, Jake ignored her question as he
rose to his feet. 'What I am planning to have, right
now, is some lunch,' he said blandly. 'So, let's go and
find it, hmm? No, not that way,' he added as she turned
towards the house. 'I decided that since it is such a
lovely day, we ought to have a picnic.'

Coming over to take her hand, he led her down a wide
flight of stone steps and across the lawn. When they
arrived at the edge of the ornamental lake, Harriet saw
that it was much larger than she had thought, with a
green island in the middle on which rested a small,
circular summer-house.

'Oh! It's beautiful!' she exclaimed excitedly, before
realising that her hand was still firmly held within his
own. 'How—how do you get across to the island?' she
asked, suddenly feeling breathless.

'Relax, you don't have to swim!' Jake grinned,
pointing to a small boat moored a few yards away.
'And before you dare to think of laughing at my lack of
prowess,' he said, helping her into the small craft and
shipping the oars. 'Just kindly remember, my dear girl,
that without me manhandling this boat, you won't get
any lunch!'

'I wouldn't dream of it,' Harriet murmured, sitting
back and letting her hand trail lazily through the cool,
clear water. The sun was blazing down out of the blue
sky, dazzling her eyes as she stared at Jake's broad
chest, and the rippling muscles of his wide shoulders
and brown arms. He certainly seemed to be an expert

rower, the oars dipping neatly in and out of the water and sending the little boat almost flying over the lake towards the island. When she said so, he laughed and confessed that he had rowed for his old college, Harvard.

Reaching the island, she found that it was harder to get out of the boat than it had been to get in. Grabbing Jake's hand, she cried out as the craft seemed to slip away from her feet, and if he hadn't seized her quickly, lifting her up on to the grassy bank, Harriet would have fallen in the water.

'I'm sorry to be so clumsy,' she murmured, suddenly realising that his arms were tightly clasped about her body. Blinking nervously, she raised her eyes to see a pulse beating rapidly in his jaw, and he was breathing heavily, his mouth parted to reveal the even whiteness of his teeth. The faintly musky, masculine scent of his body made her feel strangely dizzy, and she shivered involuntarily at the darkening gleam in his eyes.

'Six foot tall, beautiful *and* clumsy—what a combination!' he said softly.

All at once the atmosphere seemed to become highly charged with sexual tension. Her throat was suddenly dry, the blood rushing and pounding wildly through her veins as she felt the warmth of his body through his thin cotton shirt. And then he abruptly let her go, stepping back to bend down and tie the rope of the little rowing boat more securely. When he stood up again, Jake's face bore a calm, friendly expression as he lead the way towards the pretty summer house.

Of course he hadn't been going to kiss her! It was nothing but her stupid overheated imagination or, and far more likely, the effect of the hot sun and that glass of champagne, which she had swallowed so quickly back at the house, Harriet told herself firmly as she trailed slowly behind Jake's tall figure. Reaching the

summer-house, the brief scene was wiped from her mind as she beamed with pleasure at the sight of some chairs, and a round table covered with a fine damask cloth on which was placed a wicker hamper and a silver ice bucket containing a bottle of wine.

'How about some more strawberries and cream, or maybe another glass of wine?' Jake asked some time later.

'Good heaven's no! That lovely cool Muscadet on top of the champagne, has left me feeling decidedly tipsy. Not to mention the fact that I made an absolute pig of myself, gorging on your Mrs Benson's wonderful salmon mayonnaise!' She smiled, feeling sleepy and replete as she leaned back on a pile of cushions, and gazed across the lake towards where the house stood surrounded by its green lawns and trees.

They had decided not to use the table and chairs on the verandah of the summer-house. It had been so hot, that Jake had suggested having their picnic beneath the cool shade of a weeping willow tree growing beside the water, and had produced the rug and cushions from inside the small house, like a conjuror producing a rabbit.

'It's so lovely here, how can you bear to live in London?' she murmured.

'On a day like this it does seem crazy,' he agreed, lying back on the rug and placing his hands behind his head as he stared up at the pale green leaves. 'But then, life isn't composed of many halcyon days like this, when it seems a crime to do anything else but laze in the countryside. In my case, life is a four-letter word, which spells "work"!' He turned and grinned at her. 'And to enable me to carry out my business smoothly and efficiently, I need an apartment in London.'

'How did you become such a high-powered business-

man in the first place? Was it just a case of joining the family firm, or did you claw your way up the ladder, from what you Americans call "the wrong side of the tracks"?'

Jake laughed and shook his head. 'Nothing so dramatic, I'm afraid. It was my grandfather who started as a poor farm boy from the Midwest. By the time he died, I reckon he could reasonably be described as one of the major figures in international finance. As for my father . . .' He hesitated. 'I guess the fairest thing to say, is that he simply wasn't a businessman. Maybe he would have been more at home on a university campus, but it very quickly became clear that he wasn't interested and had no talent for a career in Wall Street. And that was damn nearly fatal for Lancaster International!'

There was a long pause as Jake fell silent, immersed in his own thoughts. 'So, what happened next?' she prompted quietly. Harriet was certain that he wasn't a man who often discussed his family background with anybody, let alone a girl he didn't know very well. A cynical, hard, ruthless individual, his arrogance and assurance was only partly alleviated by the charm he could turn on at a moment's notice, and the humour always lurking in those brilliant blue eyes. Apart from their first encounter, she was aware that he had deliberately sheathed his claws in his dealings with her. In fact, it was fairly amazing, now she came to think of it, that he had been so remarkably forbearing about all those items he had discovered in his apartment. And no one could have been kinder when she had been so upset about poor Mrs O'Casey. But despite giving him all credit for his leniency and restraint as far as she was concerned, Harriet had no illusions about the man lying so close beside her on the rug. She had always instinctively known that he was a dangerous man to

tangle with, and she didn't need to remind herself of her
friend Rosie's warning that to become involved with
Jake was as hazardous as playing with fire.

'What happened next was a four act drama,' Jake
said slowly. 'Advised by my mother, who has a fine,
sharp brain, my father just about managed to hang in
there and keep the wolves at bay. I joined the firm
straight from business school, and had managed to get
a grip on most of the company by the time my father,
who was coming back from inspecting one of our
factories, was killed in a plane crash. That's when the
fun started!' His lips curved into a smile of devilish
enjoyment.

'Everyone, including the whole of Wall Street and the
London Stock Exchange, imagined that Lancaster
International was up for grabs. I don't think that I've
ever worked so hard or so long in my life, but by the
end of a couple of years and after some epic boardroom
struggles, I finally managed to gain complete and full
control of the corporation. Nowadays, I spend my time
commuting between New York and London, and it's
just about been plain sailing ever since,' he added
laconically.

'What about the future? I can see that for someone of
your temperament, the battle to hang on to your
company must have been very exciting and stimulating.
But what do you do now?' she asked. 'I mean, do you
really *enjoy* taking over one company after another?
Doesn't there come a time when making more and
more money, and becoming richer and richer gets to
be . . .' she hesitated.

'Boring?' Jake gave a short laugh. 'You and my
mother would appear to view my existence with the
same jaundiced eye! She told me, not long ago, that I
was getting to be a dead bore. I wonder if she's right?'
he mused quietly.

'You . . .?' Harriet hooted with laughter. 'I can think of many things to call you, Jason Lancaster—some of which are definitely *not* repeatable!—but "a dead bore" isn't one of them!'

'Hmm. Since you, my dear Harriet, have a thoroughly reprehensible habit of telling the truth and damn the consequences, I don't think that I particularly want to hear any more on the subject of my character!'

'Oh, you're not *all* bad,' she said primly, her shoulders shaking with laughter.

'Har-ri-et!' He rolled over, raising his head and looking down into he eyes. 'You are, without the shadow of doubt, a wretched girl who is clearly destined to come to a sticky end—if I don't murder you first, that is. How you've managed to live this long, beats me!'

'Clean living and a pure heart,' she quipped lightly, the smile dying on her lips as she gazed up at his tanned face only inches from her own. His warm breath fanned her cheek, his glinting blue eyes staring intently into hers as he raised a hand to brush a lock of shining chestnut hair from her brow. It was only a small gesture, but at the gentle touch of his fingers she felt a nervous shiver run through her body.

'There is definitely something going on between you and me, but I'm damned if I know exactly what,' he said slowly. 'I'm not talking about being physically attracted to you, although God knows I certainly am. It's more than that, or at least I think so.' He frowned, looking oddly confused for a man who normally had few if any doubts about himself or his motivation in life.

Harriet stared up at him, the proximity of his broad shoulders and long, lean body creating havoc with her finely-tuned senses. She couldn't say anything, her

mouth suddenly dry and parched with tension. It seemed an age before he spoke again.

'Okay. Here's what we're going to do. Over the next two weeks I want to take you out, see a lot more of you, and . . .'

'No! No, we can't, it's quite wrong,' she said huskily, managing to find her voice at last. 'You're engaged to that beautiful model, Magda Thorne. How do you think she'll feel about your conduct? I mean, I'm hardly what she might think of as competition, but that's not the point. It's . . . well, what you are suggesting is impossible, and probably immoral as well. Surely you can see that.'

'An engagement is not a marriage,' he said firmly. 'An engagement is the time when one finds out *if* one wishes to marry that person. At this moment I don't know what I want to do,' he smiled ruefully. 'And let me tell you, sweetheart, my state of indecision is solely due to you!'

'I'm not your sweetheart,' she muttered, trying to wriggle away, but he moved his body to trap hers beneath him, catching hold of her hands and holding them firmly above her head.

'I'm taller and stronger than you are, so why don't you just relax and listen to me for a minute, hmm?' Jake smiled sardonically as he noted the anger flashing in her wide grey eyes. 'I obviously haven't been expressing myself very clearly, but what I want to say is that we basically know very little about each other. You burst into my life, Harriet, like an explosive charge of T.N.T.! And while I may have some deep, instinctive feelings about how your mind works, for instance, I still can't claim that I really *know* you—not with absolute certainty. Although, of course, in one sense, we have got remarkably well acquainted with each other, very quickly indeed!' His

lips twisted into a wry grimace as a deep flush spread over her cheeks.

'Yes, you are quite right. I do find you very, very desirable,' his voice thickened as he let go of her wrists, and slid his hands beneath the wavy mass of her hair. 'Oh, yes, I want you, and I'm damn sure that the feeling is mutual.'

'No, it isn't!' she snapped, the teeth chattering nervously in her head as she realised she must try and get out of this situation before it was too late. 'I don't know why you have this insane idea about you and me, but it's a—a load of complete rubbish!'

He gazed into her eyes for a moment, a slow smile beginning to spread over his face. Lowering his dark head, his lips gently touched first one corner of her mouth and then the other. It was a gentle, provocative caress, increasing with intensity as he savoured the sweetness of her lips with a teasing lightness that left her breathless and aching for more. A slight, helpless moan escaped from her throat at the treacherous warmth invading her trembling limbs, evoking a response she couldn't control. Frenzied shivers of excitement seemed to scorch through her body and, hardly aware of what she was doing, she slid her arms about his neck as she curved her body closer to his.

Her sensual movement provoked a low groan from his throat, his mouth becoming hard and demanding as his kiss deepened, devastating her senses and leaving her weak and helpless beneath the experienced touch of his hands as they roamed slowly over the soft curves of her body.

'Well, now . . .' Jake drawled with cynical amusement as he lifted his head and looked down at the dazed expression of the girl in his arms. 'I hope, my sweet liar, that you will now have the honesty to admit that I am

not *entirely* insane about the feelings which exist between you and me, hmm?'

Harriet closed her eyes against his mockery, but there was nothing she could do to hide the revealing tide of crimson which she could feel sweeping over her face.

'Come on, sweetheart,' Jake murmured some moments later, helping her to sit up and placing a glass of wine in her hands. 'There's nothing wrong in admitting that there's a strong, physical magnetism between us. It's something that's been around since Adam and Eve, and it's a necessary part of men and women's existence. But, as I said before, while we may be attracted to each other, there's a lot more to a relationship. I want us to get to know one another's likes and dislikes. I know nothing about your prejudices, obsessions or past experiences, for instance. Which is why I have decided that we're going to spend some time discovering each other.'

'No!' Harriet's hands trembled as she tightly clasped her wine glass. 'I've already told you why it's not possible. Quite apart from your fiancée, you seem to think you can ride roughshod over everyone. Well, I'm not a company who's prepared to be taken over—to use a metaphor that you're likely to understand—and I neither want nor need your money. So, go and play somewhere else, Mr Lancaster, because I'm simply not interested!'

He must be a good poker player, she thought, because she could never guess what he was thinking—not if he didn't want her to. 'And that's that, hmm?' he said, as if they were discussing a business matter and not something deeply personal between the two of them.

'That is *definitely* that. And I'd like to go back to London right away,' she added firmly, putting her glass into the nearby hamper.

Jake took her arm, helping her to rise to her feet on legs that felt strangely wobbly. She was nervously standing still as she allowed him to carefully remove some dead leaves which had become trapped in her cloud of wavy chestnut hair, when he bent forward to lightly kiss her ear. 'My, my, Harriet, what a challenge you are!' he whispered. 'However, it seems only fair to warn you that I always get what I want!'

Had she imagined that hoarsely whispered threat, Harriet wondered, sitting ensconced with Montmorency in the back of the Rolls Royce as Benson drove them back to London. Jake had seemed oddly distant and abstracted as they made their way off the little island and back to the house, and surprised her by instantly agreeing to her suggestion that she would prefer to be driven back to London by his chauffeur. She was sorry to have messed up Benson's day, but she knew she couldn't possibly have coped with any more of Jake's strong, dominant personality.

Asking to be dropped off at Victoria Coach Station, Harriet waited until Benson had driven away before walking slowly along the normally busy streets, which on a late Sunday afternoon were blissfully empty. Montmorency, who had obviously had a wonderful day, seemed every bit as tired and lethargic as she felt as they mounted the steps of the large house in Eaton Square. If she had hoped to sit quietly in the garden, she was doomed to disappointment. Standing in the hall, it was clearly apparent from the screeches of laughter and the loud buzz of conversation that Aunt Clarissa was giving one of her Sunday lunch parties, and that the guests were still present, filling the large downstairs rooms and lying out in deck chairs under the shady trees of the garden.

Was it any wonder that she tended to avoid this

house like the plague? Harriet thought morosely as she took Montmorency down into the kitchen. Aunt Clarissa had forbidden him the rest of the house—'such a large messy dog, dear'—and after giving him some water, Harriet trailed slowly upstairs, cursing under her breath as she was waylaid by one of the young men that her aunt was always hoping she would marry.

'I say, is that you, Harriet? You're not looking very jolly today—more like a wet weekend, ha ha!'

He looks just like a horse, and neighing down his nose like that, he sounds like one too, she thought as she nevertheless gave him a vague smile. 'Hello, Simon. Enjoying yourself?'

He leered at her. 'It's been fairly okay, but things are looking up now you've arrived. How about you and I getting together over a glass of champers, ha ha!'

From his unsteady lunge in her direction, and the way his eyes weren't focusing too well, it was clear that Simon had already had more than enough 'champers' already. Harriet had no difficulty in avoiding his arms, ducking out of the way as she began to mount the stairs to her room. 'I think I'll pass up your kind offer,' she said.

Simon wasn't too drunk to miss the dry note of contempt in her voice. 'There's no need to be so bloody superior, Harriet!' He turned as a thin, anaemic-looking blonde girl came and joined him in the hall. 'Hi, Julia. D'you know, I was only asking Harriet to come and have a drink—anybody would think I was going to rape her!' he grumbled.

'Oh, Simon, you are a hoot!' the blonde girl tittered. 'Absolutely too funny for words. Come and see mummy—she's dying to meet you!'

'Okay, yah. Why not? I'll tell you something, Julia, that girl Harriet Drummond is a right drag. In fact, I think she's worse than that—she's a bloody bore!'

Harriet missed none of their words as she rounded the stairs and walked across the landing to her suite of rooms. Stripping off her clothes, she went and had a long, cool shower before slipping on a light towelling robe, and going to sit down at her dressing table to stare blindly at herself in the mirror.

Why did she feel so alienated from the sort of people her aunt adored having in the house? It wasn't a matter of 'class', since she knew many perfectly nice, interesting people who were far better bred than she was, and had far more money as well. Maybe it was just that her aunt, who had a light, butterfly mind and prided herself on never reading a book, preferred to surround herself with the company of people who had her own level of intelligence. Simon, for instance, was Aunt Clarissa's idea of perfect husband material. The fact that he was incredibly stupid didn't seem to worry her aunt one little bit. He had a 'nice place in the country' and was connected to the dimmer half of Debrett—and that was clearly enough of a recommendation for an aunt who was becoming increasingly irritated by her recalcitrant niece. Well, she might be a drag and a bore, as far as Simon was concerned, but Harriet in turn viewed him as nothing but a pale carbon copy of a man, especially when compared to someone as strong and vital as Jake.

Trying to banish the image of that hard, forceful man from her mind proved to be practically impossible. She must forget him, she told herself desperately. It was over, finished, done with! There was absolutely no point in allowing herself to recall his lovely house, or the picnic under the weeping willow tree, and *definitely* none in remembering the scene which had followed. For some quite extraordinary, unknown reason she suddenly wanted to cry, and it seemed to take an enormous effort of will to pull herself together.

'This won't do at all,' she said aloud to her reflection, turning abruptly away from the misery that was evident in the depths of her wide grey eyes. Getting up from the stool, she went over to her chest of drawers for some clean underwear, and then put on a fresh cotton dress. She had hoped to be able to stay here, for the next week at least, because she had a healthy respect for Jake's determination to get his own way, and she knew that she wouldn't be able to totally rely on her hope that he would leave her alone. Hiding in the Eaton Square house had seemed to make sense, but not if she was going to be driven mad by the vapid company of the likes of Simon. She'd have to go back to the house in King's Cross, and take a chance that Jake wouldn't bother her. Of course, there wasn't any real need to worry. What could he do if she kept metaphorically slamming the door in his face? There was absolutely nothing to worry about—nothing at all.

Harriet never really knew why she finally succumbed to Jake's blandishments. It wasn't due to the vanload of red roses which arrived each day, nor the large, juicy bones for Montmorency that were delivered daily, fresh from the butcher. Maybe the first crack in her defence might have been the little Rockingham china castle, which was returned to her with a label attached, which read: 'My apartment is lonely and though orgies are vile, I shall go to the devil if I can't see your smile.'

She was still smiling when she incautiously picked up the telephone, something she had resolutely refused to do since she had returned to the flat, however often it rang.

'Harriet?'

She immediately recognised Jake's rich, dark tones.

'Will you please stop pestering me. I don't need any roses, and Montmorency is becoming disgustingly fat

from all those marrow bones. And the other bad news is that I'm afraid you'll never make Poet Laureate!' she said sternly, but he must have caught the note of amusement still lingering in her voice.

He gave a low laugh. 'Now that is very, very sad. I had really hoped to impress you with my classy poem. How about dinner tonight?'

'Get lost, Jake!' she answered, quickly putting down the receiver before he could say any more. But she didn't tear up the note attached to the castle, putting the china ornament on a table until it distracted her too much and she firmly banished it to the back of a cupboard.

It was probably the arrival of the elephant, which finally overcame all resistance. Harriet was having a salad lunch in her little garden, prior to her afternoon session at the law centre, when there was a ring at her doorbell. Answering it, she saw two men in buff overalls.

'Sign here, please, Miss,' one of them said, handing her a clipboard. 'And where would you like us to put the elephant?'

'The—the what ...? She looked at them in confusion.

'Wot we 'as 'ere is one h'Indian h'elephant,' the other man said, pointing to the huge crate on the street beside an enormous pantechnicon whose side bore the words: NOAH'S ARK DELIVERY SERVICE. Alongside it, in smaller letters, were the slogans: 'Large Beasts a Speciality!' and 'You Want It, We've Got It!'

'But I can't possibly ... I mean, there must be some terrible mistake!' Harriet waved her arms helplessly. 'Even if I wanted an elephant—which God knows I don't—that crate will never go through my door.'

'No problem, Miss. We sussed out the lane running

darn the side of this 'ouse, and we reckons as 'ow we can sling this 'ere crate over into yer garden.'

'No, of course you can't!' she protested angrily, but they took absolutely no notice of anything she said, and an hour later she was left with a wooden crate which dominated the small paved area, and a crowbar which one of the delivery men had left with her as an afterthought.

Two hours later, and with the combined help of all the students in the house, Harriet was left standing alone in the flat, quite unable to get back into the garden, and with the shrieks of her friend' laughter ringing in her ears. Who could blame them, she thought, gnashing her teeth with fury as she looked at the little green jade elephant lying in the palm of her hand.

On first opening the crate, it had proved to contain yet another crate inside, and so on and on, like one of the Russian dolls that tourists brought back from Moscow. Realising that it was some ghastly practical joke, she had tried to stop Andrew and the others as the piles of wood and debris mounted higher and higher. But everyone had become infected by some sort of mad hysteria: 'I'm not giving up now, Harry! There has to be *something* inside here!' Andrew had said, not pausing for a moment as he wielded the crowbar.

When at last they had come to the small, ivory box, her friends had crowded around, refusing to go until she showed them what it contained. Andrew had doubled up with laughter at the sight of the miniature jade elephant, and Harriet was still so stunned that she wasn't quick enough to stop Rosie from reading aloud the message attached to a gold chain around the animal's neck.

'Listen to this, everyone!' Rosie chortled, dodging away from Harriet's outstretched, imploring hand. '"Roses

are red ... Violets are blue ... And just like an elephant ... I can't forget you!" *Wow!* How about that for a romantic gesture!'

'It's damn well nothing of the sort!' Harriet had fumed. Eventually managing to shut the door on her friends, she marched to the 'phone. Getting Jake's secretary, Miss Norris, she demanded to speak to Mr Lancaster.

'Is he expecting your call, Miss Drummond?'

'Oh, yes. I think I can guarantee that fact!' she hissed through gritted teeth.

'Is that my sweet Harriet?' Jake was laughing as he came on the line after some delay. 'How did you like my present?'

She took a deep breath to try and steady herself. 'Your "sweet Harriet" is going out to get a loaded shotgun, and then she's going to storm your office to shoot you very, very dead—*you foul, beastly man!*'

'Calm down—there's no need to shout,' he murmured, making no effort to hide his amusement.

'Oh, yes there is! Have you any idea of the mess all those crates have made of my garden? I'll kill you, I'll ... I'll ...'

Jake swiftly interrupted her as she paused for breath. 'I think it's trade-off time, don't you? I will guarantee to remove all of the debris, if you in turn will promise to come out to dinner with me tonight. How's that for a bargain offer?'

There was a long silence as she fought against submitting to his blackmailing tactics. 'Now, Harriet, you mustn't be a bad loser,' he continued. 'What's a few pieces of wood, when I had to put up with all those birds and cats for a whole night, hmm? So, I'll call for you at eight, shall I?'

Harriet gave a heavy sigh. 'I suppose I'll have to say yes,' she muttered, putting down the 'phone before the quite hateful, most ruthless man she had ever met had a chance to laugh at her again.

CHAPTER SEVEN

'WELL now, this isn't so bad, is it?'

Harriet leaned back on the comfortable, red plush banquette seat, looking around at the Modigliani prints on the cream-coloured walls of the restaurant, and trying to avoid the sardonic gleam in Jake's eyes.

Throughout the afternoon she had been a mass of nerves, and the last half hour before he had called for her, the tension had formed itself into a hard, gnawing lump in the pit of her stomach. Choosing what to wear, normally something about which she gave little thought, had in her present state become a major problem. Twice she had changed her mind, stripping off the various dresses and hunting frantically through her wardrobe for a more suitable garment. Even now, she wasn't satisfied with the sleeveless aquamarine silk dress, with its twenties-style dropped waistline caught at her hips by a long sash, and whose brief pleated skirt only just covered her knees. It wasn't nearly as sophisticated as the dresses being worn by the other women dining here at L'Epicure, for instance. And the fact that Jake had greeted with a wolf-whistle the sight of her long, tanned legs ending in high-heeled aquamarine sandals, didn't really mean a thing. What did men know about the importance of clothes and fashion, anyway?

'Have you been here before?' His voice cut into her anxious thoughts.

'No, I haven't.' Harriet smiled briefly at a waiter as he handed her the menu, while another hurried over with the drinks Jake had ordered earlier.

'Ah, there you are. That's one of the points I was trying to make last Sunday,' Jake said. 'I had—and have—no idea of the sort of food you like, or the kind of ambiance you prefer. I will undoubtedly find out, given time, but I had to make a guess for tonight. So, in celebration of the effect you have had on my life, my dear Harriet, I decided to opt for pyrotechnics!'

She looked at him in confusion. 'I don't know what you're talking about?'

'You will!' he assured her, his blue eyes glinting with amusement. And later, watching three-foot high flames leaping from a sizzling pan as a waiter flamed the brandy sauce for her choice of *entrecôte Aphrodite*, she couldn't help smiling as she remembered his words.

'My steak is delicious, and—and it was a very good choice of restaurant,' she murmured, glancing through her eyelashes at the tall man beside her. The consumption of a dry martini before the meal, together with the subsequent glasses of wine, had helped to relax her nervous tension and forced Harriet to realise that it was both juvenile and ungracious of her to try and maintain her air of sulky grievance.

'My, my! Don't tell me that I've actually managed to do something right this week!' Jake laughed. 'Oh, by the way, you may be interested to hear that Mr Matthews is no longer a director of the Metropolitan Development company, and his brother-in-law has suddenly decided to tender his resignation from both the Planning Committee, and the local council itself. On top of which, I have been to see Mrs Peters again and given her my written assurance that neither I nor any of my companies are the slightest bit interested in the demolition of her house.'

Harriet gave him a brief smile. 'I suppose I could say: not before time! However, I am very grateful and I'm sure Mrs Peters and the rest of the people living in her

road are too. Did you have a frightful row with Mr Matthews?'

'I think that I'd prefer to draw a veil over the whole unfortunate business. However, I can say that clearing up that mess was a piece of cake when compared to the effort required to break down your resistance, Harriet. Quite frankly, I can't think of anyone—male or female—who has *ever* given me such a hard time.' He shook his head sorrowfully.

'You've got a nerve saying that!' she said indignantly. 'What about me, for heaven's sake? I never want to see another red rose as long as I live, while as for that nonsense with the elephant . . .! And you can wipe that grin off your face, right this minute!'

'But I thought you loved animals?' Jake assumed an expression of injured innocence that didn't fool her for one minute.

'Animals, yes. But a one-inch, small jade elephant, buried inside I don't know how many crates of wood —no!'

'Aw, come on, Harriet! I spent hours trying to think of something that would make you laugh, and quite a few days arranging all the details. Confess now, it was a good caper, wasn't it?'

'Yes, well . . .' Her lips widened into a reluctant grin. 'It wasn't quite as good as my budgerigars, of course, but on the whole I would agree that you show a promising talent for creating mayhem and chaos!'

'I shall take that as a rare compliment from an expert in the field,' he murmured, his shoulders shaking with amusement. And then they were both roaring with laughter. So much so that the other diners in the restaurant raised their heads at the sounds of hilarity issuing from the dark corner where Jake and Harriet were leaning against each other, helpless with mirth.

'Where—where did you find that appalling Noah's

Ark Delivery Service?' she asked, wiping away her tears of laughter. 'And that awful man who kept going on about "h'Indian h'elephants" . .'.

'Do you mind?' he said indignantly. 'It was all my own brilliant inspiration. Getting hold of the van, and arranging for it to be sprayed, lettered and so on, was no problem. Neither was employing those two out-of-work actors—I'm glad to hear that they put on a good performance! No, it was finding someone to make all those crates that was the real problem.' He turned his head and gave her a warm smile. 'Still, you're now sitting here beside me, so I guess it was worth all the effort.'

Feeling suddenly nervous at the pronounced gleam in his eyes, and the underlying, serious tone to his light words, Harriet looked down at the tablecloth as she fiddled with her wine glass. She couldn't think of any light or amusing conversational gambit, certainly nothing that wouldn't sound unsophisticated or inane. So she opted for the truth.

'I—I didn't think that I would enjoy myself tonight,' she said slowly. 'But it has been fun and, under . . . well, under different circumstances I'd like to have seen you again. However, it really has to be the last time, Jake.' She raised her wide grey eyes to his. 'I—I can't stop you doing any more crazy things to get me to go out with you, but I hope you won't, because it's not something that I'm going to find funny any more. I wouldn't be honest if I didn't admit that I'm flattered you've gone to so much trouble to see me. But I don't like hurting other people, and if I was Magda, I'd be feeling very hurt and upset by your behaviour. Please try and understand,' she pleaded.

'Hmm.' Jake's face was inscrutable as he called for the bill and led her from the restaurant.

Sitting in the car as he drove her back to her flat, the

silence seemed deafening. It wasn't a long journey, but every minute seemed to last an hour, and when Jake brought the vehicle to a halt she didn't know what to do, longing to flee indoors and yet not quite able to summon the courage to do so.

'I find myself in a difficult position,' Jake said quietly, staring straight ahead out of the windscreen. 'I must tell you that Magda has been delayed in Brazil, the modelling contract taking far longer to fulfil than she had thought. Since last Sunday, I have been trying to speak to her, to tell her that I want to terminate our engagement, but the telephone service in South America is diabolical, and I haven't managed to get hold of her.' He gave an exasperated sigh.

'I'm not the cowardly sort of man who is given to writing a "Dear John" letter. Withdrawing from our engagement is something that I must talk about to Magda, in person. However, for maybe the next two weeks it isn't going to be possible. So, what do I do? Avoid you like the plague until I'm technically free? It's ridiculous!'

Harriet had been holding her breath while he had been speaking, and now she was filled with a most peculiar mixture of elation and depression. 'I—I honestly didn't mean to cause trouble between you and Magda,' she muttered. 'Maybe, when she comes back . . .?'

'No,' he said firmly. 'It isn't your fault, or only in so far as I realised that it was no good settling down with one woman, when I wanted to see a lot more of another. Maybe, I'm just not the marrying kind, hmm?' He gave a harsh bark of laughter. 'However, I'm damned if I'm going to waste time pussyfooting around until Magda gets back to England—life's too short for one thing, and I'll have to fly off to New York on business soon, for another. So, how about it?'

'I don't know . . .' She hesitated, not knowing quite how to answer him. Things between them were obviously going to be based on a different footing if he wasn't engaged to Magda any more, but Harriet wasn't sure she could cope with Jake's high-powered, ruthless invasion of her life, nor with what he might expect of her. He and Magda had obviously been having a rip-roaring affair, and the beautiful model was undoubtedly only one of a long string of women with whom he'd had a sexual relationship. Since she, herself, was lamentably naïve and had never even been to bed with a man, it all sounded a recipe for disaster. What had they in common, after all? Maybe it would be better—and safer—if she called a halt to any further involvement right now.

Jake leaned an arm along the back of her seat, placing his hand on her shoulder and drawing her gently towards him. 'Just relax, sweetheart, hmm? There's no need for you to get all up-tight, nor to tell me that you're an innocent, old-fashioned type of girl, because I already know that,' he murmured softly, his warm breath fanning her cheek as he lifted a stray lock of her hair and gently tucked it behind her ear. She shivered at his touch, trembling as his fingers moved to turn her head to face him, staring mesmerized at the eyes glinting down at her in the dim light of the street lamp. 'So, we'll play it your way, nice and slow, and take our time to get to know each other, okay?'

'You—you don't m-mind . . .?' she stammered breathlessly.

He smiled, his teeth gleaming in the darkness. 'I'm a normal, red-blooded male, and you are well aware of the fact that I find you very desirable—something that we both confirmed last Sunday, hmm?' He paused as he raised a finger to gently trace the outline of her quivering lips. 'There are any number of women with

whom I could engage in a bedroom romp, if I was so minded. However, my sweet Harriet, it's you that I want and fully intend to have. So, however long it takes—I guess I can hack it!'

He lowered his head, his mouth brushing her temple before sliding down to tease the edge of her lips, parting them with a sensuously gentle kiss that made her ache for more. 'It's time you were in bed, you gorgeous girl—and I only wish it was mine!' he whispered, reluctantly giving her a brief kiss before getting out of the vehicle and coming around to open her door. 'I have to fly to Scotland tomorrow, but I'll be back in time to take you out to dinner again,' he promised, waiting until she had let herself into the house, before getting back into his car and roaring off into the night.

Harriet floated around her flat in a mindless daze, not really able to comprehend what was happening to her. His image filled her dreams and haunted her all the next day until, as he had promised, he appeared on her doorstep at the appointed hour.

Despite running a large, international business, Jake seemed to have unlimited time at his disposal, time which he insisted on spending with her. Harriet spent hours trying to convince herself that she was too young and too inexperienced to interest him for long, quite apart from the fact that they had nothing in common; but he seemed impervious to any of her hesitant suggestions that maybe they should see less of each other, constantly expressing nothing but pleasure in her company. Each succeeding day, she became more and more torn between the deep feelings that Jake was evoking within her, and the certain knowledge that there could never be any future to their relationship. The tension, and the strain of being well aware that Jake was handling her as he would a trout on the end of a line, allowing her a feeling of freedom while slowly but

inexorably reeling her in towards him, might have proved too much for her to bear if a different aspect and dimension hadn't entered into their close involvement with each other.

'Quite honestly,' Harriet told Montmorency, one morning as she sat drinking her coffee while the dog snuffled in a dark corner of the garden, trying to remember where he had buried a bone. 'I've never had quite so much *fun* in all my life!'

It had started when Jake had called her one day to fix a date for the evening. She had been bubbling with excitement, having heard that morning that she had passed her final law exams with flying colours. 'That's great news!' he had said, and asked her to decide where they should go to celebrate the event. Harriet had thought hard and long, and had finally decided on something she'd never done before: to have an evening cruise on the Regent's Canal, a waterway carved through Regent's Park at the beginning of the 19th century to service the commercial pressures of the Industrial Revolution. Jake had gone completely mad, and had hired a narrow boat fitted out as a cruising restaurant, just for them alone. It had been a wonderful, magical evening, and sipping her wine as they drifted slowly down the canal, she had asked him whether there was anywhere that he, too, particularly longed to visit.

'Well,' he paused to consider the matter. 'I guess I've seen most of the tourist sights—the changing of the guard, Buckingham Palace—all that sort of thing. I bet I probably know more about London than you do!' he teased.

'Oh, yeah!' she grinned vulgarly. 'I'll accept that bet, because I'm sure you don't know where you can buy American postage stamps and have a drink, at one and the same time!'

None of his suggestions were correct, and Harriet left him guessing until the next evening, when she took him to The Mayflower pub in Rotherhithe Street. As they drank their beer and looked out of the porthole windows, she explained that the famous ship had been moored nearby, before setting sail for Southampton and the New World. When it returned in 1621, the master of the ship had died and been buried in Rotherhithe, and in honour of the close connection with the United States, the pub was licensed to sell both British and American stamps.

'Okay—one up to you,' Jake laughed. 'But just wait and see, I'll get even!' And that had been the start of an amazing few weeks. Jake had taken her to see John Keats' house in Hampstead, where she shed a tear over the manuscript of *Ode to a Nightingale*, written by the man who had so tragically died of tuberculosis at the early age of twenty-six. As a complete contrast, she had suggested greyhound racing at Haringey, were they watched the dogs tearing around the track as they ate fish and chips, after which Jake had come up with tickets to watch tennis at Wimbledon, plying her with strawberries and cream until she felt ready to burst.

And so it had gone on. They had taken a boat down the Thames to Hampton Court, visited the real elephants at the London Zoo, hunted for antiques in the Portobello road, watched *A Midsummer Night's Dream* at the Open Air Theatre in Regent's Park and, at Jake's instigation, had spent a ghoulish hour wandering through the London Dungeon, whose slimy vaults and horrifically recreated scenes of medieval torture and murder made Harriet feel quite sick. To punish him, she had taken him yesterday to spend a whole afternoon sitting on a hard bench at Lord's Cricket Ground.

'I don't think he was very impressed with our

national game of cricket!' she told Montmorency, wondering if that was why Jake had looked so grim when he had dropped her off at the flat in the late afternoon, and hadn't made a date for that evening. Maybe it was just that he had work on his mind—he'd certainly been neglecting his business for the last weeks. 'And he definitely doesn't care for you!' she added with a laugh, as Fred flew down to perch on the arm of the bench seat, feeding the parrot some sunflower seeds before leaning back on the soft cushions and soaking up the early morning sun.

Yes, they'd had a lot of fun together, she thought, sighing as she realised that like all good things, it must soon come to an end. She hadn't dared to prick her bubble of happiness by asking Jake when Magda was due to return, but it must be very soon, and there was no way she could possibly compete with the American girl's cool beauty and high level of sophistication. Quite apart from the worrying, unresolved question of Magda, and just how Jake would feel when he saw her again, Harriet was under no illusions about her own emotions—or that Jake's intentions were strictly dishonourable.

She had managed to keep her head—so far. But as the days passed, and she fell more and more in love with him, it was becoming increasingly difficult to resist Jake's subtle blandishments. His kisses had changed from a simple caress to that of a far deeper and disturbing erotic experience. The situation seemed to be slipping out of her control and had now become a subtle battle of willpower, the sensual torture of unsatisfied fulfilment keeping her awake night after night, as she relived the exquisite, thrilling sensations engendered by the mastery of his experienced lips and hands. Never could Harriet have dreamed that she was capable of melting with such pleasure in a man's arms.

Never before had she been so shockingly aware of just how easy it would be to succumb to the intensity of her emotions, completely losing sight of the harsh fact that she was living in a transitory dream-world which had no basis in reality.

Her reverie was interrupted by the ring of the telephone. Jake's voice was brisk and she could hear the rattle of a typewriter in the background. 'We're going out for the day. I'll pick you up in half an hour, okay? 'Bye.'

'Hang on a minute,' she said breathlessly as he was about to put down the phone. 'What about your business? You can't keep on neglecting your work like this!'

He laughed. 'You'll be glad to hear that today's outing is strictly legitimate. I have to go down to see the managing director of a computer company I own, near Worthing. So, I'll complete the business, and then we'll have lunch and go for a walk on the beach. Hurry up and get ready, because I'm leaving the office right now, okay?'

Quickly changing out of the jeans she was wearing, and putting on a brightly checked skirt and matching short sleeved cotton blouse, Harriet swiftly made arrangements for Montmorency to be looked after by the boys in the massage parlour next door. They were devoted to the dog, spoiling him outrageously and feeding him totally unsuitable food, but it wouldn't hurt for one day, she told herself as she heard Jake's impatient toot on the horn.

'It doesn't look very good weather for beach-combing,' she said, settling into the passenger seat of the Ferrari and squinting up at the dark storm clouds obscuring the blue sky.

'Nonsense! I've put the fix in, and it's going to be a lovely day,' Jake assured her with a smile as he let out the

clutch and the super-charged engine roared down the street.

'I don't think much of your talent for masterminding the weather,' Harriet shouted some hours later. It was difficult to make herself heard over the loud rattle of hailstones on the tin roof of the deserted beach hut, where they had run for temporary shelter from the storm which had been threatening to break all day.

'You're right, I must be losing my touch,' Jake agreed, taking off his soaking wet jacket and looking at her drenched, shivering figure with concern. 'We'll have to do something, otherwise you'll probably get pneumonia. I guess our best bet is to make a dash for the car, and then aim for Dragons which isn't too far away. At least you'll be able to have a hot bath and a change of clothing, although goodness knows whether I've got anything that will fit you.'

'I'm not fussy,' she assured him through chattering teeth. 'Just lead me to that hot bath and I'll be your friend for life.'

'What a promise! Why didn't I think of taking you out in a hail storm before now?' he laughed, taking a firm grip of her hand as they ran across the shingle beach towards his car parked on the headland.

A warm bath, when you're feeling desperately wet and miserable, must be one of the really great experiences of life, Harriet thought, lying back in the fragrant hot water and savouring the luxurious feel of the bath oil as it coated her long-limbed body. Her teeth had been chattering too fast for her to talk much during the journey to Jake's country house, but she had noted that his immaculate hand-made suit was every bit as soaking wet as her blouse and skirt. She had told herself that while her need was great, maybe she ought to let him have the first bath; which had been stupid of her, she

now realised, since this huge house seemed to have at least one bathroom for each of the seven bedrooms, and no doubt others in the staff quarters as well.

Reluctantly deciding that she couldn't stay in the bath for ever, Harriet slowly climbed out and towelled herself dry, before putting on the cream silk dressing gown Jake had handed to her as he had shown her into one of the guest suites. Belting its sash about her slim waist, she looked around the large room, noticing that there seemed to be a hair-drying appliance hooked up on the pale blue tiled wall. The opportunity to dry her wet hair, and so look less of a drowned rat, was irresistible, and twenty minutes later as she contemplated her appearance she decided that she felt slightly more confident. She could have done with some lipstick, of course, but the bathroom cabinet had proved to be empty of anything other than a bottle of aspirins and some cotton wool.

Opening the door and entering the bedroom, whose pale blue and white decor echoed that of the bathroom, she found herself wondering if Magda had used the silk dressing gown and this particular suite of rooms in the past. But there was no sign of anyone's occupancy, male or female, and then as she looked out of the window across to the ornamental lake, Harriet castigated herself for being so foolish. Magda would have shared Jake's room, of course. Where else would that cool, sophisticated woman have slept, but with the master of the house to whom she had been—and maybe still was—engaged to be married?

'This is a bad scene, and you've got to get out of here!' she said aloud, feeling suddenly foolish as she realised that Montmorency, her constant companion to whom she so often talked aloud, was spending the day back in London.

Quickly gathering up her wet clothes, she went out on

to the landing and on down the stairs to the large panelled hall. Hesitating for a moment, she looked through the various, beautifully decorated rooms, finally opening a door to discover a book-lined room with a log fire burning in the grate, and Jake sitting in a black leather arm chair.

'Feeling better?' he asked, putting down the papers he had been studying and rising to walk over to an oak cabinet. 'Come on in, you look as though you need a brandy,' he added as he produced a decanter and two glasses.

'I—er—I wonder if you have a tumble drier . . .?' she muttered nervously, trying to tear her gaze away from the sight of Jake's tall figure clothed in a dark blue, short towelling robe which amply displayed his tanned, hairy chest and his long mahoghany-coloured legs.

'There's no problem about that,' he said, coming over to take the wet clothes and place a glass of the amber liquid in her hand. 'I'll take these out to the kitchen, while you go over and sit down by the fire.'

'I hope your Mrs Benson doesn't mind drying my clothes?' she said as he returned a moment later.

'I'm sure she wouldn't, if she was here. But since it's her and Benson's day off, the question is an academic one. However, I'm a big boy now, and quite capable of operating a simple piece of machinery on my own!' Jake smiled as he came over and sat down beside her on the large couch upholstered in soft, rust-coloured suede. 'You look frozen. Drink up,' he insisted. 'It's just what you need to warm you up.'

'It's far too early . . .' she protested weakly, but as he twisted his body towards her, placing an arm along the back of the couch and giving her a warm yet mocking smile, she buried her face in the glass. Harriet wished he wouldn't smile at her like that, as though he was well aware of how nervous she felt sitting here with him in

an empty house, and with virtually nothing on except the thin silk dressing gown. She could feel the hot colour rising to cover her cheeks, as she realised that he must also be naked beneath his short towelling robe.

A silence fell in the room, the only sound being the flicker of the flames and the crackle of logs in the grate. Harriet sipped her brandy, staring blindly into the fire. Every single one of the physical sensations she experienced whenever she was alone with Jake, had returned to assail her more fiercely than ever. Why was it that only with him she should feel her heart pounding so rapidly, her skin burning and then shivering as if she had a chill, her ears almost deafened by the sound of the blood racing around her body?

'Magda has returned from Brazil, and we had dinner together last night,' Jake said coolly, moving his fingers to toy with a lock of her chestnut hair.

'Oh ... yes ...?' Harriet could feel herself tense, trying to control her trembling hand as she lifted the glass of brandy to her lips.

'Yes.' He continued to play with her hair, his blue eyes noting her rigid figure without comment. 'We had a long, frank talk and we both decided that we weren't suited to a permanent relationship. It was all very friendly and amicable. So that's that.'

'I'm—er—glad she wasn't upset ...' Harriet murmured, moistening her lips which had suddenly become dry and parched, and evading his eyes as she continued to stare into the fire.

'So am I!' He gave a low laugh before asking abruptly, 'Tell me, Harriet, have you ever been in love?'

Dear God! What on earth was she supposed to say? If only she could tell him she loved him more than life itself; that knowing he didn't love her was a torture she was coming to find almost unbearable, and that she despised herself for not being able to draw away from

the magnet of his physical presence. 'I—I don't quite know what you mean.' she said in a small voice.

'Well, it has occurred to me that while we have seen a great deal of each other during the last weeks, and I've told you all about myself and my family, you have been remarkably close-mouthed and silent. No details of your parents or family background, for instance. Nothing about your past love life—and don't tell me a beautiful girl like you hasn't had any boy-friends, because I would find that impossible to believe!'

'Ah ... well, yes, I'm sure I've told you that my parents died when I was twelve. After that, I was brought up by an uncle and aunt. They are very boring and you wouldn't be interested in them,' she said hurriedly, trying to whip her mind into overdrive and find something with which to distract him from pursuing his present train of enquiries—this was definitely not the time or place to tell him the truth about her background. 'As for my love life ... well, it has hardly been extensive ...'

'At your age, I should hope not!' Jake murmured drily. 'However, I'm agog to hear all the riveting details!' he added, and when she hesitated, he buried his fingers in her hair, turning her face towards him. 'Shoot!'

She winced at both his firm grip and the steely tone in his voice. 'Please let go of my hair, you're hurting me,' she muttered. 'However, if you're hoping to hear something that would warrant an "X" Certificate, then I'm afraid you're going to be disappointed,' she added huskily, wishing that he wouldn't look at her like that, his hard mouth twisting into a smile that made her pulses race and her body go weak with longing.

'I expect I'll be able to stand the excitement, so quit

stalling, hmm?' he said softly, removing his fingers from her hair and clasping her trembling hands together in his.

'I—I've had a lot of boyfriends, of course, but nothing very serious—just people to go out and enjoy myself with, that's all.' She paused for a moment. 'Yes, I suppose there was someone who I thought I was in love with. He was very nice, very suitable, and had all the right qualities—at least I thought he had. However, I—er—decided one day not to see him again.'

Jake waited to hear if there was any more to the story, and when it was clear that there wasn't, he frowned. 'Are you saying you gave him up—just like that?'

'Just like that.'

'But why? What had he done?' Jake tilted his head as he considered her in silence for a moment. 'Was his lovemaking too rough for you?' he asked softly.

Harriet shook her head. 'No, nothing like that.' She hesitated. 'I really don't want to talk about it. It was only an infatuation that immediately died the death one day, when I overheard him telling a friend of his the reason why he wanted to marry me. And that's all I'm going to say,' she added mulishly, clamping her lips together.

'Hmm. What about Andrew?'

'What about him?'

'Oh, come on, Harriet! One look at you and that boy together, and it was clear he was mad about you.' Jake said impatiently.

Cursing inwardly as she felt herself blushing, Harriet forced herself to meet his eyes. 'I didn't know that was how he felt—not until the other day. And—and I told him it was no good. He doesn't like Fred either,' she added inconsequentially, a faint smile curving her lips.

'I'm not surprised, that bird's a bloody menace!' He

gave a harsh bark of sardonic laughter. 'Well,' he said after a few moments' silence. 'I guess that just leaves the question of you and me, hmm?'

He moved closer on the couch, still keeping hold of her wrists as he drew her slowly towards him. 'No . . .!' she gasped and then suddenly he had both his arms around her, holding her firmly as he lowered his dark head to stare intently into her eyes.

'If you're going to say "no", you'll have to sound a lot more convincing than that, my darling,' he whispered as his mouth found hers and she melted beneath the kiss which her traitorous body had been craving for hours. Weakly winding her arms about his neck, she abandoned herself to the deep sensual need which gripped her, a need so intense that it obliterated all thought, all caution. She could have lain in his arms for ever, and when their mouths parted and he lifted his head, she couldn't prevent a soft moan of disappointment issuing from her lips.

Giving her another swift kiss, Jake rose in one fluid movement from the couch, lifting and holding her in his firm embrace. He carried her swiftly from the room, up the stairs and along the landing. She was still trying to gather her scattered wits, to break out of the miasma engendered by his close proximity, when she felt him pause to kick a door open and the next moment she found herself lying on a large bed. She was trembling violently as he stood looking down at her glowing, chestnut hair spread out over the gold brocade bed-cover, and she saw his blue eyes widen, their glittering brilliance becoming cloudy and sensual as they roamed over her slim figure. The very air of the room seemed to hang suspended, the moments stretching endlessly as she lost all awareness of herself; hypnotised by the compelling message conveyed by his eyes, she became oblivious of all sense of time and space. She stared up

at him, her eyes remaining locked with his as he swiftly unbelted and tossed aside his robe, lowering himself down beside her and taking her into his arms.

Harriet lay as if in a trance, feeling the warmth of his body through the thin layer of her silk gown, and savouring the masculine, musky scent of his warm skin. Jake slowly trailed his lips over her forehead, his kisses hot on her eyelids before moving down to delicately touch a corner of her lips.

With tantalising slowness, he explored her soft mouth with gentle yet sensual kisses that set the blood pulsing warmly through her veins. His moist, firm lips gradually became more insistent, his kiss deepening as he sensuously and erotically explored the inner softness of her mouth. She felt as though she was drowning, drifting way out of her depth as she buried her fingers convulsively in his dark hair, dizzily responding to the fast, irregular beating of his heart so near her own, and the increasing, urgent hunger in his lips.

Slowly and reluctantly Jake raised his head. She heard his sharp intake of breath as he looked down at the girl lying in his arms, at the trembling temptation of her lips and the fluttering lashes as she gazed blindly back at him, totally enmeshed in the trance-like thrall of overwhelming passionate desire.

'Harriet . . .!' he whispered, his pounding heartbeat and ragged breathing clear evidence of his arousal as with slow, unhurried movements he released the loose sash at her waist, his fingers gently parting the sides of the flimsy silk gown to expose her breasts to his view. As he lay looking down at her, Harriet felt as though her breath were suspended somewhere in her throat. Her heart was beating and pounding with a heavy choking thud, her body shaking and quivering and her mouth so dry that she was forced to moisten it with the tip of her tongue. A shudder ran through his long body

at her action, his breathing unsteady and his hands shaking as he slowly removed the silk gown, his mouth tracing its passing with lingering pleasure. She gasped nervously, realising that nothing in her limited experience had prepared her for the earth-shattering effect of his slow, featherlight touch, and the resulting tidal wave of sexual excitement as his lips seductively caressed her skin.

'My sweet, darling . . .' he breathed, savouring every moment as his long tanned fingers moved leisurely over her warm, pliant flesh towards the aroused and tormented peaks of her breasts, swollen and aching in anticipation of his touch. He suddenly groaned, lowering his head to press his face to her soft, fragrant skin, his mouth hotly possessive against the deep valley of her breasts, and she realised that she wasn't afraid of the unknown as she had feared she would be; that she was fiercely exultant, almost swooning from the sharp current of pleasure that ran through her body like forked lightning as he cupped her full breasts in his hands, hungrily kissing the hard, tumescent points. She cried out at the flood of desire flowing swiftly through her veins, and as his touch grew more urgent, more possessive, her whole being began to vibrate in response to his sensual arousal as he trailed his lips over the smooth skin of her stomach, his fingers softly caressing her inner thighs and producing an extraordinary, heart-stopping pleasure that she could not have believed existed.

'So lovely!' he murmured thickly, moving his body to cover hers. 'So lovely and unawakened . . .' The feel of his hot flesh against her was exquisite, and her overwhelming compulsion was to respond to her clamouring urge for his hard, strong male body. Moaning with submission, she moved sensually beneath him, innocently and instinctively inviting his invasion.

'Please, Jake ... please ...!' she gasped, arching wantonly against him, her body turned to molten fire, burning and craving his possession, her total, erotic abandonment making it increasingly difficult for him to control his leashed strength. The breath rasped in her throat as she sobbed his name in a mindless refrain, before the intense, tingling pleasure which had been filling her body suddenly exploded deep within her.

A deep, husky growl was torn from his throat, her sweet moistness enveloping him as he slid between her thighs. Beneath his thrusting body, she became a wild creature that matched him in the elemental, wildly primitive storm of passion that rocked them both; her pain dimly felt and then forgotten as pleasure exploded yet again and again inside her in convulsive waves until, all passion spent, Jake's warm arms enfolded her and she floated slowly back down to earth.

They must have both fallen asleep, because when she opened her eyes again she saw through the window that the rainstorm had passed over, now replaced by the feeble rays of a watery, late afternoon sun. Harriet felt a hand sliding over her skin, and turning her head she saw that Jake was awake, his warm smile broadening as she gasped at his explicit touch.

'Sweet, lovely Harriet,' he whispered, his strong arms tightening possessively as he gently drew her against his hard, firm body. 'How gloriously soft your flesh is— smooth and soft as silk.'

She buried her face in his shoulder, not knowing what to say—well, what did people say after they had been making love? Despite her overwhelming feelings for Jake, he had given her no sign, no indication that he felt for her anything other than a strong physical attraction. It was obvious that he was a very experienced lover, and it would be stupid of her to expect him to regard their passionate lovemaking as anything more

than an enjoyable encounter. The fact that she had never known anything like it before, and that for her it had been a wonderful, fantastic, and totally mind-blowing experience, probably only went to show how naïve she was.

She gave a slight, unconscious sigh as she recalled her instinctive knowledge that she shouldn't become involved with this man. He had made her feel too much. His lovemaking this afternoon had been so fiercely passionate that it had marked her for evermore. She knew with absolute certainty that he was the first and the last for her; that if there was to be only this one time with him, she would still never, ever want another man.

'Harriet?' he murmured, turning her flushed face towards him and gazing deep into her eyes. 'What's wrong, sweetheart, hmm?'

'Nothing, I . . .' she gave a shaky, trembling smile. 'I obviously haven't—I mean, I don't know what one's supposed to do now.'

'Ah, well . . .' he drawled silkily, trailing his mouth over her eyelids and down her cheek to claim her soft, quivering lips. The tantalising sweetness of his kiss caused a sudden flame of passion to rage through her trembling body. She was aware, with a dizzy sense of elation, of his quickening arousal and that his heart was beginning to beat as rapidly as her own.

Jake slowly lifted his head, looking down at the beautiful girl in his arms. 'It shouldn't take you very long to guess *exactly* what we're going to do next!' he smiled, his voice thick and husky with desire.

'But you surely can't . . .'

'Oh, yes, I can!' he growled with amusement, his arms tightening about her slim figure. As he bent to possess her lips once more, there was a sudden clattering and buzzing sound that almost made her jump out of her skin.

'Hell and damnation!' Jake swore loudly, releasing her before getting up off the bed and going through into an adjacent room. Mystified, Harriet wound a sheet around her naked figure, and followed to find him standing in a small room by a machine that seemed to be spewing forth strips of paper.

'What is it?' she asked, looking at the machine in puzzlement.

'Trouble at t'mill, as you say in Britain—or more precisely in this case—trouble in New York! I'll have to get back to London quickly. What's the time?' He strode past Harriet who was standing in the doorway, pausing to give her a brief kiss before walking over to pick up his watch from the top of a chest of drawers. 'Hmm, six o'clock, so it's still only two o'clock in New York. I might just make it if we get our skates on. Sorry, darling,' he turned to smile at her. 'I've got so much to say to you, but it will have to wait until I've contacted my New York office. So, jump into your clothes as quickly as you can—at least they should be dry by now—and then we'll be off.'

'I could have telexed to New York from Dragons,' Jake explained as they neared the outskirts of London. 'However, I'm having to go to the office, because I need to check some names and figures in the files there.'

'What's happening in New York?' she asked, still feeling dazed by their lovemaking and the speed of their departure.

'Some two-bit banking outfit seem to think that they're in a good position to take over one of my companies. Oh, boy—are they in for one hell of a surprise! By the time I've finished with them, they'll be a lot sadder and wiser, believe me.'

Harriet did indeed believe him. She didn't need to hear his hard, ruthless tones or to look at the militant, angry blue eyes to know that she felt sorry for the

people who had the temerity to oppose Jake Lancaster. She shivered slightly and snuggled down in her seat.

'I really am sorry about this, sweetheart.' He turned to smile at her, casting his temporary fury aside as a snake would slough a skin. 'I'm not going to take you home, because we've still got a lot of talking to do. I'll drop you off at my apartment, and give you the keys so that you can let yourself in, okay? It's Carter's day off, and there'll be no one to disturb you. Just fix yourself a drink and I'll be along as soon as I can. I'm sure that it's only going to be a matter of half an hour or so.'

'Well, I really should collect Montmorency from the massage parlour . . .'

'Oh, God! I keep forgetting about that awful place. Surely the dog can wait for his supper just this once, can't he?'

'Yes, I suppose so.'

'Good girl,' he murmured, slowing down outside the large modern apartment block. 'Here are the keys,' he said, placing a small bunch in her hands. 'Now, out you hop and I'll be back as soon as I can, okay?' He didn't wait for an answer as he waved and drew the Ferrari back out into the traffic.

It took Harriet some minutes of trial and error to work out which of the keys opened the front door of Jake's apartment. Shutting the door quietly behind her, she walked down a long passage and into a simply huge room which seemed to be composed mostly of windows. Going over to the wide expanse of glass, she was amazed by the wide, panoramic view of London which lay spread out before her. Turning to look around the room itself, she wrinkled her nose at the stark modern decor. Jake had never brought her back to his apartment for some reason, and she now felt glad that he hadn't done so. If he had asked for her

opinion of the decorative style, she would have been hard put to say anything polite!

Turning back to the window, she inadvertently knocked over a tall, thin object which fell to the parquet floor with a clatter. Bending down to pick it up, she heard a voice calling from somewhere in the large apartment. Puzzled, since Jake had said that it was Carter's day off, she moved in the general direction of the sound, looking in one empty room after another. She was just about to open a door on one side of the hallway, when the voice called again, and she turned to see that a door opposite was ajar.

'Cooee ... I'm in here, Jake, darling!' the voice called.

Confused, Harriet walked over and pushed the door open, her eyes widening with shock as she saw that it was a large bedroom, and on a mammoth-sized bed on the far side of the room was lying ...*a completely nude woman!*

'Oh, hello! What are you doing here, sweetie?'

Harriet's eyes blinked rapidly, her vision clearing as she realised that it was Magda Thorne who lay stark naked on what could only be Jake's bed. The lovely model made no attempt to cover herself, stretching languorously as she gave Harriet a brilliant smile.

'It was *terribly sweet* of you to look after darling Jake for me, while I've been away,' she purred. 'I told him last night that I really didn't mind if he wanted to have himself a little fun on the side! However, now I'm back, and after that wonderful, absolutely terrific time we had making love last night ... he's such a strong, vigorous lover, isn't he? Well, little girl, I'm afraid you'll just have to go back and play with kids of your own age, hmm?'

Harriet was too stunned to do or say anything. She stood paralysed in the doorway as Magda slowly got up

off the bed, and went to stand in front of a long floor-length mirror. Humming happily to herself, the model turned this way and that, running her hands slowly up and down over her figure as she admired the reflection of her naked flesh. 'Darling Jake always claims that my breasts are perfect,' she murmured. 'What do you think, hmm . . .?'

At long last, Harriet managed to break out of her shocked trance, a sharp, painful cry breaking from her throat as she turned to rush blindly down the corridor, Magda's triumphant peals of laughter resounding and echoing around her ears.

CHAPTER EIGHT

IT must be one of the hottest summers on record, Harriet thought, walking slowly across the buttercup-strewn meadow whose long grass was still damp from the early morning dew, and stopping to wave to a group of Piers' farm workers gathering up the hay bales in one of the adjacent fields. She'd always loved this particular part of East Dorset known as the Isle of Purbeck. Not that it was an island, of course, just a wide peninsular bordered on the north by Poole Harbour and on the east and south by the English Channel, but the area with its small grey stone villages, little stone hamlets and minor roads and tracks, still seemed to have preserved the qualities of a bygone age, when time moved at a far slower pace and was light years away from the frantic, noisy hustle and bustle of modern Britain.

Montmorency tugged sharply at his long lead as a rabbit darted out of the grass and ran away up the footpath ahead of them, growling with acute frustration at not being able to give chase. Harriet felt sorry for the dog, but she was forced to keep him on a lead ever since he had proved to be so unreliable with the farm animals, snapping at the heels of the Friesian cows and frenziedly barking at Piers' beloved sheep, before chasing the poor creatures all around the fields. She still shuddered at the memory of her cousin's furious reaction to such canine hooliganism, and the tongue-lashing which had followed.

'You'd better keep that hearth-rug of a dog under better control, because the next time he scares my

sheep—it will be the knackers' yard for old Montmorency!' Piers had thundered angrily.

'Piers didn't mean to be horrid,' Caroline had said as Harriet sat feeling depressed and gloomy in the large farmhouse kitchen. 'He's just particularly up-tight at the moment, because he's hoping that his beloved Dorset Horns will win a prize at the Royal Show next week. Not that he's really got a chance, but I wouldn't dream of mentioning the fact!' she added with a laugh. 'Come on, Harry. Stop moping and help me to pick some peas for supper.'

Harriet had blown her nose and willingly agreed to help her old schoolfriend. Piers and Caroline had been so kind and comforting when she had unexpectedly turned up at Old Abbey Farm three weeks ago, accepting without comment both her sudden appearance and the hastily fabricated, unconvincing story that she'd been forced to leave London because her flat was being redecorated. Not that Caroline had for one moment believed such an unlikely tale, especially since it was only a few months ago that she had gone up to London for the weekend, expressly to help Harriet spring-clean and repaint the flat. But after one glance at her friend's forlorn, unhappy figure and the taut misery etched on her lovely face, Caroline had quickly choked back anything she might have been going to say, merely giving Harriet a warm hug and welcoming her into the house.

After that terrible discovery of Magda Thorne—not only lying stark naked on Jake's bed, but also so avidly and greedily awaiting his return—Harriet had rushed from the apartment with such speed, it wasn't until she found herself standing out on the street in the middle of Park Lane, that she managed to break partially through some of the shock and horror which was gripping her mind and body. Dazed and trembling, she leaned

against the large plate glass windows of a car showroom as she tried to force herself to think about what she was going to do. The overriding impulse which surfaced in her disorientated, stunned mind was that she must get as far away from Jake as she possibly could.

Hailing a taxi, she had arrived back at her flat only to find that she must have thrown her own keys away with those belonging to Jake, when she had rushed pell-mell out of his apartment. Tim and Geoffrey, the boys in the massage parlour, had come to her rescue and they couldn't have been more kind and comforting to the girl who was so obviously suffering from deep shock and distress; Tim brewing up a hot cup of tea while Geoffrey climbed over the wall and broke into her flat through the kitchen window. Promising to look after Fred and Clarice, they had tried to persuade Harriet that she wasn't in a fit state to drive anywhere. But she had adamantly insisted that she must leave London, and after throwing some clothes into a suitcase, she had led Montmorency around to a side street where her small car was garaged.

It wasn't until some hours later, when she was travelling along the M3 motorway towards the Worthingtons' estate in Dorset—the only place where she had ever been really happy, and where she knew that Jake would never find her—that the full implication and significance of all that had happened that day suddenly hit her. Shaking and shivering, she was forced to pull quickly off the road, dashing out of the car and over to some bushes where she was immediately and violently sick.

There was no doubt that she had been taken for one of the biggest fools alive. How could she have been so crass, so credulously stupid and idiotic as to believe one word of what Jake had said? Sitting on the side of the

motorway, she bowed her head in her hands, but there was nothing she could do to expunge the sight of Magda from her brain. Magda, whose nude, voluptuous body had lain so temptingly and invitingly on Jake's large bed. There was no possible way of misinterpreting what she had seen, absolutely no doubt that far from having broken off his engagement, Jake was still as firmly tied to his fiancée as he had always been.

'A little fun on the side' was how Magda had referred to Jake's determined pursuit and courtship of Harriet, and the bile rose once more in her throat as she realised that was all she had ever been: a momentary diversion in his busy life, a small challenge to his masculinity. Rosie had warned her in no uncertain terms, and she had also been well aware that she wasn't the first and wouldn't be the last woman in Jake's life. He'd had a past, to which she'd been foolish enough to think that Magda belonged, and she had always known, despite her hopeless love and wild, impractical dreams, that there was no possible future for two people from such totally different backgrounds. But finding Magda in his bed in London, only hours after Jake had made love to her at his home in Sussex, had been such an appalling revelation of his duplicity, such a perfidious, nauseating betrayal, that she almost fainted from the pain and agony.

Every day of the interminably long, desperately unhappy three weeks which had passed since she had fled from London, had only served to increase her hopeless love and longing for Jake. Despite her certain knowledge of just what a double-dealing, immoral and two-faced swine the man was, her days and nights seemed haunted by his charismatic presence. Calling him all the names under the sun didn't seem to have the slightest effect on her emotions, and although she told herself she would get over him and the way he had

treated her, that one day she would wake up and be cured of this lovesickness, it hadn't happened yet.

The only way she could keep sane was to take long, exhausting walks that left her too tired and worn out to do more than fall into bed each evening, and which also had the virtue of keeping her away from the farm. Not only was it the busiest time of the agricultural year for her cousin and his wife, and a girl who knew nothing of practical farming was worse than useless, but Caroline was clearly finding it extraordinarily hard not to ask some searching questions. Especially after last night when she had found Harriet crying in the kitchen.

'Thank goodness it's only you—I thought we had burglars!' Caroline said, frowning as she looked up at the kitchen clock above the warm Aga cooker. 'My God, it's two o'clock in the morning! What's wrong? Are you feeling ill, Harry?' she added, looking with concern at her friend's slim, trembling figure.

'No, I'm fine,' Harriet mumbled, turning aside to brush away her tears. 'I just felt like a cup of cocoa, that's all.'

'Hmm . . .' Caroline paused for a moment and then came over to put her arm around Harriet. 'I honestly don't want to interfere,' she said tentatively. 'But you're obviously unhappy, and I'm sure it would help if you could talk to someone about whatever it is that's making you so miserable.'

But Harriet hadn't been able to face explaining, even to such a good friend as Caroline, just how foolish and silly she had been to fall for Jake Lancaster's blandishments. Pride might well be a sin, but it was all she had to cling to at this dark time in her life and despite her friend's kind intentions, she insisted that she'd only been downstairs for a drink and some aspirins for a headache, returning upstairs to lie awake for the rest of the night.

Coming down to breakfast this morning she had
found Piers in the kitchen, fresh from feeding his
animals and hungry as a hunter himself. Caroline's
pregnancy meant that she sometimes didn't feel too
well early in the day, and so Harriet had fallen into
the habit of cooking her cousin's breakfast. As she
whipped the scrambled eggs and fried the bacon, she
had been astonished when Piers had put down his
paper and announced that he thought she ought to see
a doctor.

'You're looking damned peaky, Harry. Don't want
you coming down with 'flu, or something worse.'

'Has Carrie put you up to suggesting this?' she asked,
and from the faint blush in his cheeks, she saw that her
suspicions were correct. 'Relax, there's nothing wrong
with me that staying away from London won't
eventually cure. So just be a good cousin and eat up
your breakfast,' she said firmly, putting the plate down
in front of him.

'Didn't want to interfere . . .' he muttered with his
mouth full. 'Caroline thinks . . .' but he had no chance
to say any more as his wife burst into the kitchen.

'Honestly—that mother of yours, Piers! She always
was a bit odd, but now I think she's going round the
bend! I just rang her up to give her the gynaecologist's
report—well, you know how she's been panicking about
the new baby—but she wasn't the slightest bit
interested. I couldn't make out what she was so excited
about, but it seemed to have something to do with the
Wars of the Roses and golden goose eggs! I told the
silly old trout . . . sorry darling, but your mama really is
getting as nutty as a fruit cake . . .!' Caroline laughed
and kissed the top of her husband's head. 'Anyway, I
kept telling her that we didn't have any chickens, let
alone geese, but I don't think she heard a word I was
saying.'

'Probably getting senile dementia,' Piers murmured, looking at an article in the Farmer's Weekly. Harriet was momentarily amused to note that he was clearly far more interested in a new sheep dip, than in his parent's possible loss of her mental faculties.

'Well, I don't know . . .?' Caroline gave the question some serious thought. 'She certainly didn't need any prompting to remember that Harry's staying with us. In fact, your Aunt Clarissa sends you lots of love,' she said, turning to grin at Harriet. 'You are definitely the flavour of the month! She kept on saying what a too-too wonderful, darling girl you are, and she always knew that you would do the right thing in the end!'

Harriet gave her a wry smile. 'That doesn't sound a bit likely. Maybe Piers is right, after all.'

Caroline shrugged and sat down to nibble some dry toast. 'Well, from the way she was going on—and goodness knows the old girl was confused—anybody would think that you'd made her utterly and supremely happy by winning the football pools for your Uncle Ralph *and* deciding to marry one of those awful men she's always pushing your way.' She laughed, and added nonchalantly, 'I suppose you're not thinking of getting hitched to that "Hooray Henry", Simon Molyneux, are you?'

'Hardly! That really would be a fate worse than death!' Harriet said lightly, getting up from the table and picking up the small picnic basket she had prepared earlier. She realised that if she stayed any longer in the kitchen, Caroline was going to begin cross-questioning her about last night's tearful episode and knowing her friend as she did, she hadn't been deceived by that nonchalant reference to Simon. Caroline was obviously convinced that problems with a man lay behind Harriet's present unhappiness, and that was a line of questioning that she could do without.

Piers looked up from his magazine. 'Where are you off to, today? Well away from my sheep I hope!'

'Don't worry, Montmorency is a reformed character—especially on the end of a lead! I thought we'd walk to Corfe Castle. It's not far, and has always been one of my very favourite places.'

'Don't be back too late,' Caroline said, clearly disappointed at not being able to have a heart-to-heart talk with her friend.

She was going to have difficulty in heading off Caroline's curiosity about exactly what was wrong with her, Harriet realised, as she and Montmorency approached the steep, grassy hill on which was perched the old ruined castle, towering high above the village whose houses of grey Purbeck stone sparkled in the morning sun. Since there was no way she could bear to tell the unvarnished truth about her relationship with Jake, maybe it was time she returned to London. If she had been able to think at all rationally during her precipitous flight from Jake's apartment, she would have realised that there was no need to have sought sanctuary down here in Dorset. Once Jake had returned and seen Magda, he would have known that it was pointless to see Harriet again. Not that he would be interested in doing so, of course, since he had only been interested in getting her into his bed—and having achieved that, he would have soon been off, seeking some other stupid young girl who needed her wits examined.

Sighing heavily, Harriet slipped the dog off his lead as they reached the summit of the hill. Pleased to find that they were quite alone in the deserted ruins, she found a warm grassy corner of the ramparts and sat gazing out over the fields and woods of the countryside which lay spread before her like a patchwork quilt. Sharing her picnic with Montmorency, she cudgelled her

weary brain, trying to decide whether to go back to London, or to stay on with Piers and Caroline for a little while longer. Quite apart from the fact that she really ought to be making some decisions about whether to become properly articled to a solicitor, it was becoming increasingly obvious that she must find a job that absorbed most if not all her waking moments.

That old cliché, about time being a great healer, was proving to be utter nonsense. During the last three weeks there hadn't been the slightest diminution of her intense longing for Jake's presence, the aching need for the caress of his hands on her body. She'd even, one dark and lonely night, almost picked up the telephone and called his apartment, so desperate had she been for the sound of his voice. Luckily, she had clung on to her sanity by the skin of her teeth, and resisted the stupid urge to make yet more of a fool of herself than she had already. She must, she really must decide what to do. If only she didn't feel so tired . . .

It was the excited barking of a dog that broke through the heavy mists in her brain, and some moments later Harriet slowly opened her eyelids to realise that thanks to her lack of sleep last night, she had dozed away in the hot sunshine. It must have been Montmorency who had been making all that noise, she thought, struggling to sit up. There weren't likely to be any sheep up here, of course, but she didn't want him making a nuisance of himself by teasing anyone else's dog. Turning to look about her, she saw that Montmorency was licking the hand of someone sitting on a fallen lump of masonry, and her body suddenly became taut and rigid with shock.

The sickening, apprehensive lurch in her stomach left her feeling as if she was in a lift that was hurtling down from a great height. Blinking rapidly, her eyes dazzled as she stared into the blinding rays of the full

afternoon sun, Harriet had difficulty in clearly seeing the features of the man, but there was no mistaking those broad shoulders, nor his great height as he rose to his feet and walked towards her.

'Go—go away . . .!' she managed to whisper as she found her voice at last.

'Go away? After all the damn trouble I've had tracking you down? You must be joking!' Jake said forcefully, putting out a hand and jerking her to her feet.

'Leave me alone! I d-don't want to have anything to d-do with you,' she stuttered, trying to pull away from the fingers firmly gripping her arm.

'I've got to talk to you,' he said, ignoring her violent struggles to evade him. 'It's taken me three weeks to find you, and I'm sure as hell not letting you out of my sight until I'm good and ready to do so!'

Harriet felt almost faint, barely able to stand on legs that felt as weak as water. Why hadn't he left her alone? Okay, so she hadn't been very successful in her attempt to forget the man who had meant so much to her, but she had at least been trying. Now, here he was, the force of his strong personality once more closing around her. Jake had a total conviction that he could always get what he wanted, and unlike other mortals, he didn't seem to be able to accept the possibility that he couldn't have his own way all the time. She knew enough about him to recognise that his tenacity was formidable, and it took all the limited power at her command to defy him once more.

'We have absolutely nothing to say to each other, except goodbye! Just looking at you makes me feel sick to the pit of my stomach. Why don't you go back to your fiancée and leave me alone?' she cried. 'As far as I'm concerned, you two disgusting, immoral people

deserve each other, and ... and I fervently hope you both rot in hell!'

Jake greeted her furiously angry words with a sardonic smile. 'I've certainly been in hell for the last three weeks. However, I have a great deal to say to you, and nothing—*absolutely nothing*—is going to stop me. So while I admire your spirit,' he added in a voice of steel, 'I suggest that you calm down and let me explain a few things.'

'There's no need to explain anything. I already *know* just what a fool I was to get involved with a two-faced, professional seducer like you!' she snarled. 'I can't imagine why you've bothered to try and find me, since all I ever meant to you was another notch on your bloody bedpost. And take your damn hands off me!' she yelled, almost beside herself with fury as she struggled in vain to escape the fingers that were now biting into her arms like talons.

Jake's eyes became as hard as granite. 'I have no intention of leaving without us having a long talk,' he said loudly and slowly as if speaking to someone who was deaf. She raised her chin defiantly, but all the time she was aware of his hands pulling her closer and closer, and strive as she might there seemed to be nothing she could do to stop her weak, traitorous body from being drawn inexorably towards him, her heart beginning to pound like a sledgehammer as their bodies finally touched.

'Please leave me alone ...' she protested, and Jake gave a low laugh.

'But it doesn't please me to leave you alone!' he mocked, and then he prevented her from saying any more as he ruthlessly crushed her body to his hard chest, his mouth possessing her trembling lips in a kiss of scorching intensity that made the blood leap and race through her veins. She tried to cling to sanity. To

remember just how he had cold-bloodedly made love to her while his mistress-cum-fiancée had been waiting for him, lying naked on the bed in his London apartment. But her own emotions defeated her, betraying her in a vortex of whirling passion, forcing her surrender to the sensual enslavement of his lips as their bodies fused together, vibrating as an answering drum to his demanding kiss; his touch and his very closeness wrapping her in liquid fire as she melted helplessly in his arms.

It was an age before Jake raised his head, and as their lips parted, Harriet leaned against his broad chest still shuddering from the force of their mutual passion. Dazed and helpless, she could summon no resistance as he led her across the grass, firmly sitting her down on a stone slab that was warm from the heat of the sun.

'It's nice to know that when you get argumentative, I'll always be able to kiss you into silence,' Jake murmured softly, gently brushing a lock of hair away from her forehead. 'Now, first of all, I want to make it very clear that whatever you saw in my apartment—or anything Magda may have said to you—was utterly and absolutely false!' He looked intently down into her dazed eyes. 'Are you listening to me, Harriet?' he demanded, giving her a rough impatient shake when she didn't immediately respond.

Harriet could only nod dumbly, her mind still trying to cope with the shock of his sudden appearance, and that devastating kiss.

He sighed heavily. 'I don't quite know where to start this damn story, but I suppose the whole sorry mess began with my mother. Not that it really had anything to do with her, of course . . .' Jake frowned, pausing for a moment as if to marshall his thoughts. 'The fact is, I called to see my mother one day, and in the course of our conversation she accused me of not only being in

danger of becoming a workaholic, but a bore as well.'
He shrugged. 'I guess she had a point, and maybe it got
under my skin, because when she said that I needed a
wife, also mentioning that she would like a grandson or
two, to carry on the family business, I decided to take
her advice.

'I'll freely admit to you, Harriet, that there was no
one special in my life at that time. Okay, so I had lots
of girlfriends, but that was all they were, whether I slept
with them or not. However, once my mother had
broached the subject, I gave the matter some thought. I
saw that I'd been working so damned hard all my life
that although I had always fully intended to get married
some day, and settle down to raise some kids, I had
somehow always been too busy to do anything
constructive about it. Flying all over the world isn't
exactly conducive to serious courtship, and although I'd
met lots of nice, attractive, suitable girls, my life was so
peripatetic until the last year or so, that it was always a
case of "Hello", and then "Goodbye". If ever I thought
about it, which was seldom, I guess I considered that
my lifestyle was no basis for a serious relationship.' He
shrugged his shoulders and fell silent for a moment.

'However, following my mother's pep talk, I thought,
why not? Why not find a suitable girl who'd make a
beautiful wife and a good mother? I suppose it sounds a
bit cold-blooded, but other than when I was in my
teens, I had never been what is euphemistically known
as "in love". It had always seemed to me to be a
particularly tiresome emotion, leading to all sorts of
dramatic upsets and traumas, which I could well do
without—*and how right I was!*' Jake added with
considerable feeling. 'Anyway, I looked around and
Magda seemed to fit my requirements, so I asked her to
marry me, and if I thought about my future, it was in
rosy terms of a quiet home life with a couple of children

in the fullness of time, and no disturbance to my way of life.'

Harriet wriggled on the stone bench. 'I don't really see why you're telling me all this,' she murmured, her frozen mind and body slowly coming back to life.

'Just listen and you'll hear how Jake Lancaster got his come-uppance!' he said with a self-derisory bark of harsh laughter. 'I have omitted to mention that my mother had also given it as her opinion that what I needed was someone, and I quote, "to ruffle my feathers'. In other words, someone who would disturb the calm tenor of my life. I may tell you that the idea was not one that I welcomed, and in getting engaged to Magda, I was opting for a situation I knew I could control at all times. And then, just as everything seemed set fair for a quiet, peaceful life, what happened? That quite crazy, extraordinary girl, Harriet Drummond, burst into my life with all the peace and quiet of an atomic bomb—*that's what happened*!'

Jake rose to his feet and paced up and down the grass sward, brushing his hands roughly through his dark hair. 'Jesus—I couldn't believe it! There was this six foot tall girl, looking like something from some rent-a-weirdo agency, demonstrating outside my office, causing mayhem at the Annual General Meeting of the company and lecturing me on my moral duty to an old woman, and I—who had clearly lost temporary leave of my senses—thought she was the most gorgeous thing I'd ever seen! I couldn't keep my hands off her, and despite everything she did, and however outrageous she was—not to mention that horrendous parrot who should have been strangled in the egg—I fell more and more desperately in love with her every passing day!'

Harriet stared in open-mouthed shock at Jake who seemed oblivious of her presence, almost forgetting her as he continued to pace up and down. He didn't really

mean . . . he wasn't really in love with her, was he? She didn't have time to think clearly, as Jake began speaking again. 'And then, oh boy, was I in trouble! I'd just got engaged to Magda and then—*wham!*—I was in love, really in love, for the first time in my life, with another girl. Not that I didn't fight against it, because believe me, I did! It wasn't until that Sunday, after we'd had our picnic on the island and you firmly turned me down, that I realised I didn't give a hoot in hell for Magda—or any of the other women I'd ever known. That what I felt for you really was love with a capital "L", and if I didn't move fast I was going to lose the only girl in the world for me. It was a situation of nightmare proportions, and for the first and only time in my life, I couldn't think what to do. Eventually, I got my act together and realised that you weren't the sort of girl who was prepared to fool around with a man who was engaged to another woman.' He turned to stare intently at Harriet. 'So I had to tell Magda that I'd changed my mind. Only, she was in Brazil and I couldn't get in touch with her. I knew I couldn't bear not to keep on seeing you, and yet there was no way of formally cancelling my engagement. All I could do was to assure you that my involvement with Magda was off, dead, finished, and impatiently count the days until she returned to Britain.'

He came over to sit down beside her and took her trembling hands in his. 'I was so in love with you, but for the first time in my life I was terrified of losing someone who had become so precious. Those weeks we had together, exploring all the different, unusual places in London, was a magical time for me and I hope for you too. Also, for the first time in my life, I was able to forget business, losing any interest or desire to keep on making money for its own sake. We were having such

wonderful, uncomplicated fun, which was something
I'd never known before, and I couldn't bear the
thought that it would ever end. However, Magda
duly returned from Brazil, and so I took her out to
dinner to break the news of my change of heart.' He
sighed heavily. 'It was not, as they say, a good scene.
I didn't want to worry you, so I told you everything
was fine and we were pledged to remain good
friends. Unfortunately, that wasn't true. Magda took
it far harder than I realised she would, and stalked
out of the restaurant breathing hell-fire and brim-
stone.'

'But ... but she told me you'd spent the night
together. And when I saw her lying naked on your
bed ...'

Jake gritted his teeth and swore under his breath.
'You'd think a man of my experience would have
remembered to ask for his keys back, wouldn't you?'
He shook his head at his own folly. 'Darling, I promise
you that I did *not* spend the night with her, but stayed
quietly at home in my apartment celebrating the fact
that she'd walked out of my life for ever and—if I'm
going to be totally honest—in the joyful anticipation of
taking you to my bed just as soon as I could. God
knows, I'd been going mad with frustration, but I knew
that to make love to you while I was technically
engaged to Magda, would have been quite wrong.' He
sighed heavily. 'How could I possibly have imagined
that Magda would plan a last ditch attempt at a
reconciliation by appearing stark, staring nude in my
bed? Who, in their right mind, would dream of doing
such a thing? And since I'd told her that I was madly in
love with you, how on earth she imagined that I would
be at all sexually interested in her, I have absolutely no
idea!'

Harriet had been listening very carefully, and the

strong note of sincerity in his voice was unmistakable.
The full realisation that he hadn't been two-timing her
as she had thought, made her heart sing and she felt
quite dizzy with joy. She looked down at her hands, still
tightly clasped in his, as a disturbing thought occurred to
her. 'How ... how did you know ... I mean, what are
you doing down here?'

'You wretched girl! Why in the hell didn't you tell me
the truth about yourself, and save us both from these
last weeks of such unhappiness?' He stared down at her,
his eyes searching her face which had suddenly gone
blank, her slim figure stiffening as the import of his
words struck home. He gave a heavy sigh. 'Thanks to
your crazy family set-up, sweetheart, I've had a terrible
time getting through to the facts of the matter. After I'd
arrived at the apartment and found that you weren't
there, I shook the truth out of Magda before throwing
her out on her ear. I subsequently found your keys on
the floor of my living room, and worried sick I high-
tailed it around to your apartment to find that the birds
had flown—literally. As soon as I saw that Clarice and
wicked Fred weren't in residence, I knew you wouldn't
be back for a bit.' He gave a harsh laugh. 'I had all the
kids in the house down and put them through the third
degree, but none of them was any help, except that cute
little blonde girl, Rosie. After I had convinced her of
my pure intentions—and that took some doing!—she
volunteered the strange information that she had a
feeling you weren't all you appeared to be. "She's got
someone or something else in her life" was that shrewd
girl's assessment, and she advised me to contact
London University for any further details. Yes, you've
guessed,' he laughed harshly. 'The damn place is
virtually closed for the summer. However, after chatting
up the admissions secretary, she came up with an
address of a bank in the city: Drummond and Harley's,

to be precise. And that, my sweet, is when I began to
use my head, at last. All those shares you had in my
company? That appearance at a City banquet? The
Rolls Royce in which you left the Mansion House?
Believe me, you couldn't have kicked me any harder
than I kicked myself! However, the bank were as
close-mouthed as the proverbial oyster, and although
I knew I could put enough pressure on at least one of
the partners to make him divulge further details, I
wasn't able to because I had to fly off to America on
urgent business. I nearly went mad, but there was
nothing I could do until I returned to Britain.
When I did so, I found out that dear old Carter had
known all about you from the beginning! I nearly
throttled the stuffing out of him when he took pity
on my maudlin state and "told all" as they say in
the best novels. After that, it was merely a question
of popping around to see your uncle and aunt
and . . .

'Aunt Clarissa . . .!' Harriet looked at him in
astonishment. 'You don't mean to say you've actually
been to see her? I don't believe it!'

'I can assure you that your aunt was delighted to
meet me, and was totally bowled over by my charm,' he
said smugly.

'Hah! I don't believe it, she can't stand Americans,'
Harriet retorted.

'Ah, yes. Well, honesty does compel me to add that
my money did have just the teeny-weeniest effect on her
viewpoint.' He smiled cynically. 'That, and my complete
assurance that she and your uncle can continue to enjoy
their lifestyle and that house in Eaton Square when we
are married . . .'

'Oh, my goodness! So that's why she was so
hysterical on the 'phone to Caroline this morning. The
"wars of the roses" and goose eggs must have meant

York and Lancaster—Jake Lancaster, the goose that lays golden eggs, to be precise. Piers is right, anyone who can get that muddled must be senile!' she laughed, before recalling what he had also said. 'No, Jake. It's no good talking about marriage, because it simply wouldn't work out.'

'I've never heard of anything so ridiculous! I love you, and I'm as damn certain as I can be, that you love me, hmm?' He lifted his hand, and slowly turned her face to him. 'My sweet, Harriet,' he breathed, and she could feel his fingers shaking with the hunger and longing that was evident in his hoarse voice, and in the eyes that reflected back her own desperate need of him. 'I don't believe you can tell me, honestly to my face, that you don't love me. God knows, I may well regret the years of experience behind me,' a faint tinge of colour reddened his cheeks and his voice became thick and husky. 'However, I do know that when we made love, not only did I find in your sweet arms something I've never experienced before: a mystical blending of body and soul that far transcended anything or anyone I'd ever known, but also—and just as important—that you had unreservedly given me your whole heart. Surely you cannot mean to deny that, my darling?'

Harriet flushed. 'Yes, well I do care for you . . .'

' "Love . . .", Harriet,' he corrected her firmly. 'L.O.V.E. Say it—the word won't bite you!' he shook her lightly. 'My darling girl, you have a heart like a hotel and pour your love out on your animals and on the poor and needy, so why deny it to me?'

'I—you don't understand!' she protested helplessly. 'It just wouldn't work, that's all.'

'Why, because you are a rich girl, and you feel you must somehow sublimate that fact by giving it away to the needy?' He shrugged. 'That's okay by me. I've got

plenty for us both, for heaven's sake!'

'But we're so different! We have absolutely nothing in common—nothing at all. Your family might hate me, for instance, and ... and I'm not damn well prepared to live in that ghastly apartment of yours. Not only because of all your other women, but also for the simple reason that I really hate the decor!'

Jake threw back his head and roared with laughter. 'God, you're priceless, Harriet, you really are! Who cares about the damn apartment? I certainly don't, and I agree that it's decorated in a terrible style. I was very involved in a take over battle when I bought the place and just handed it over to some smooth, fast talking interior designer, and told him to get on with it.' He took her hand and pulled her to her feet, leading her slowly across the grass. 'In fact, you'll be glad to hear that I have already placed it in the hands of an estate agent, and I have particulars of various places that you might like to live in, instead. For instance, there's a very nice place in The Boltons, with a large garden, which seems ideal.'

'No, I can't live with you. We're simply too different. What do we really know of each other ...'

'Well, I for one know a great deal about you, Harriet. For instance, I can guess that the reason you so precipitately gave up your previous boyfriend, was because he was only interested in your money—right?' He waited until she gave a reluctant nod, and then continued. 'I am also aware that you have a most extraordinary complex about being "naïve" and "un-sophisticated", which is absolute nonsense when you're such a knock-out, both mentally and physically. What else? Oh yes, if I know that busy little mind of yours, you've been wondering if Magda and I had made love at Dragons—and the answer is, no. Come on, confess,'

he gave her a broad smile, 'I'm not doing badly, am I?'

She threw him a shame-faced grin and looked quickly away. 'No, I suppose you're doing quite well, actually.'

' "Actually"! I'm crazy about your accent,' he laughed, and then paused. 'Okay, I'll tell you something else, although you may not like to hear it. When you're a bit older, sweetheart, you'll realise that in trying to get away from your Aunt Clarissa and leading your crazy double life, only meant that you fell between two stools. That you were neither one thing or another, and consequently didn't feel one hundred per cent settled in any way of life. *That* was why your animals have always been such a comfort—you knew where you were with them, didn't you? And *that's* why my heart was in my mouth too many times for comfort, because at any moment you could have decided that I wasn't "safe", and turned your back on me and retreated to a life of service to others in denial of your own emotional needs and desires.'

Harriet leaned against the comfort of his broad shoulder for a moment, realising that he did know her, almost better than she knew herself. 'Yes, I'll admit that a great deal of what you say is right, but we really have nothing in common, do we?'

'I don't believe that a girl of your intelligence can be spouting all this garbage!' Jake exploded. 'How stupid can you get?'

'I'm not stupid!' she retorted stiffly.

'No? Then how come you haven't realised that we are *very* alike, hmm? That's the first thing I noticed about us, for God's sake! Who else has the strength of character to stand up and give me hell—and get away with it? We've both come from the same banking

background, albeit on different sides of the Atlantic, and as for my mother . . .' he grinned. 'I called to see her when I was in America, and told her all about you. I can promise you that I haven't seen her laugh so much in years! She thinks you sound great, and has made me promise to give you her love and to tell you that if you keep on ruffling my feathers for the rest of my life, you'll make her a very happy woman. So she approves, Aunt Clarissa and Uncle Ralph are over the moon, we'll have a new house of our own, and it shouldn't take you very much longer before you'll come to realise that you can't cure all the ills of the world. That, like the rest of us, you have to accept the responsibilities that money brings, and just do your damnedest to help those who are less fortunate than yourself. There's no reason to wear a hairshirt because your father left you a great deal of money, darling,' he said quietly. 'If you want to give it all away, that's fine by me. Or you can found a trust for poor old ladies who find themselves homeless, or whatever.'

Buried deep in thought, Harriet looked up to see that while she had no recollection of how she'd got there, they were standing by his car on the road below the castle, and Montmorency had somehow managed to get himself into the back seat of the vehicle.

'Now there's a smart guy who thoroughly approves of me!' Jake said, turning to face her. 'Well Harriet— what other damn fool objections are you going to come up with now, hmm?'

'I can't possibly . . . my cousins at the farm . . .'

'No problem, my love. I called there earlier today, just after you'd gone for a walk, in fact, and had a long chat with your friend Caroline. I regret to tell you that she thinks you'd be mad not to snap me up while the going's good!' he grinned.

'My God—you fancy yourself!' Harriet scowled at him.

'Not half as much as I fancy you,' he retorted with a wolfish smile. 'I promised that we'd return to open a bottle of champagne and have an early supper at the farm, after which I fully intend to drive as one possessed back to Sussex for a long, long night of hot, passionate lovemaking. Now, you wretched and most beloved girl, I dare you to look me in the eye and tell me that you aren't interested in my wicked proposition!'

Harriet could feel the hot colour sweeping over her face. The man was quite impossible, but she really had to make one more effort to try and bring him to his senses. 'What about Fred?' she asked.

Jake groaned. 'Do I have to include him in the deal?'

'Fred and I are very good friends,' Harriet said primly, trying not to smile at the look of horror on Jake's face.

'Okay,' he said at last. 'Let's have a trade off. I'll put up with Fred—although I fear he will make me an old man before my time—but only on one condition. That before we get to Sussex, you will boldly and unequivocally tell me that you love me to distraction, and that you will faithfully promise to love, honour and obey me, just as soon as I can lay my hands on a special marriage licence. How about it?'

'Well ...' Harriet paused, looking at the man she loved so much, and realising from the slight shake in his hands and the pulse beating fast at his temple that Jake Lancaster, that widely feared, ruthless tycoon was, for probably the first and only time in his life, uncertain about the outcome of a deal. She took a deep breath. 'I must say that I'm not *entirely* sure about the word "obey",' she murmured, before

giving him a broad smile. 'However, my darling Jake, I imagine that we can negotiate that point, and sort out any other details in the small print of the marriage service by the time we reach Sussex, don't you?'

Harlequin Presents

Coming Next Month

Available in September wherever paperback books are sold, or through Harlequin Reader Service:

In the U.S.
P.O. Box 1397
Buffalo, N.Y.
14240-1397

In Canada
P.O. Box 2800, Postal Station A
5170 Yonge Street
Willowdale, Ontario M2N 6J3

**Could she find love as a
mail-order bride?**

MARIANNE
WILLMAN

PIECES
OF SKY

In the Arizona of 1873, Nora O'Shea is caught between
life with a contemptuous, arrogant husband and
her desperate love for Roger LeBeau, half-breed
Comanche Indian scout and secret freedom fighter.

Harlequin "Super Celebration" SWEEPSTAKES

NEW PRIZES—NEW PRIZE FEATURES & CHOICES—MONTHLY

1. To enter the sweepstakes, follow the instructions outlined on the Center Insert Card. Alternate means of entry, NO PURCHASE NECESSARY, you may also enter by mailing your name, address and birthday on a plain 3″ x 5″ piece of paper to: In U.S.A.: Harlequin "Super Celebration" Sweepstakes, P.O. Box 1867, Buffalo, N.Y. 14240-1867. In Canada: Harlequin "Super Celebration" Sweepstakes, P.O. Box 2800, 5170 Yonge Street, Postal Station A, Willowdale, Ontario M2N 6J3.

2. Winners will be selected in random drawings from all entries received. All prizes will be awarded. These prizes are in addition to any free gifts which might be offered. Versions of this sweepstakes with different prizes may appear in other presentations by TorStar and their affiliates. The maximum value of the prizes offered is $8,000.00. Winners selected will receive the prize offered from their prize package.

3. The selection of winners will be conducted under the supervision of Marden-Kane, an independent judging organization. By entering the sweepstakes, each entrant accepts and agrees to be bound by these rules and the decision of the judges which shall be final and binding. Odds of winning are dependent upon the total number of entries received. Taxes, if any, are the sole responsibility of the winners. Prizes are not transferable. This sweepstakes is scheduled to appear in Retail Outlets of Harlequin Books during the period of June 1986 to December 1986. All entries must be received by January 31st, 1987. The drawing will take place on or about March 1st, 1987 at the offices of Marden-Kane, Lake Success, New York. For Quebec (Canada) residents, any litigation regarding the running of this sweepstakes and the awarding of prizes must be submitted to La Regie de Lotteries et Course du Quebec.

4. This presentation offers the prizes as illustrated on the Center Insert Card.

5. This offer is open to residents of the U.S., and Canada, 18 years or older, except employees of TorStar, its affilliates, subsidiaries, Marden-Kane and all other agencies and persons connected with conducting this sweepstakes. All Federal, State and local laws apply. Void where prohibited or restricted by law. Winners will be notified by mail and may be required to execute an affidavit of eligibility and release which must be returned within 14 days after notification. Winners consent to the use of their name, photograph and/or likeness for advertising and publicity in conjunction with this and similar promotions without additional compensation. One prize per family or household. Canadian winners will be required to answer a skill testing question.

6. For a list of our most recent prize winners, send a stamped, self-addressed envelope to: WINNERS LIST, c/o Marden-Kane, P.O. Box 525, Sayreville, NJ 08872.

No Lucky Number needed to win!